THE QUICK
AND THE THREAD

WITHDRAWN

JUN – – 2011

AN EMBROIDERY MYSTERY

THE QUICK AND THE THREAD

AMANDA LEE

WHEELER
CHIVERS

This Large Print edition is published by Wheeler Publishing, Waterville, Maine, USA and by AudioGO Ltd, Bath, England.
Wheeler Publishing, a part of Gale, Cengage Learning.
Copyright © Penguin Group (USA) Inc., 2010.
The moral right of the author has been asserted.

LIBRARY OF CONGRESS CATALOGING-IN-PUBLICATION DATA

Lee, Amanda, 1967–
   The quick and the thread : an embroidery mystery / by Amanda Lee.
     p. cm. — (Wheeler Publishing large print cozy mystery)
   ISBN-13: 978-1-4104-3185-1 (pbk.)
   ISBN-10: 1-4104-3185-1 (pbk.)
   1. Needleworkers—Fiction. 2. Craft shops—Fiction. 3. Women merchants—Fiction. 4. Murder—Investigation—Fiction. 5. Embroidery—Fiction. 6. Oregon—Fiction. 7. Large type books. I. Title.
PS3620.R4454Q53 2011
813'.6—dc22   2010040020

BRITISH LIBRARY CATALOGUING-IN-PUBLICATION DATA AVAILABLE

Published in 2011 in the U.S. by arrangement with NAL Signet, a member of Penguin Group (USA) Inc.
Published in 2011 in the U.K. by arrangement with NAL Signet, a division of Penguin Group USA Inc.

U.K. Hardcover: 978 1 408 49419 6 (Chivers Large Print)
U.K. Softcover: 978 1 408 49420 2 (Camden Large Print)

Printed in the United States of America
2 3 4 5 6   15 14 13 12 11
ED132

THE QUICK
AND THE THREAD

CHAPTER ONE

Just after crossing over . . . under . . . through . . . the covered bridge, I could see it. Barely. I could make out the top of it, and that was enough at the moment to make me set aside the troubling grammatical conundrum of whether one passes over, under, or through a covered bridge.

"There it is," I told Angus, an Irish wolfhound who was riding shotgun. "There's our sign!"

He woofed, which could mean anything from "I gotta pee" to "Yay!" I went with "Yay!"

"Me, too! I'm so excited."

I was closer to the store now and could really see the sign. I pointed. "See, Angus?" My voice was barely above a whisper. "Our sign."

THE SEVEN-YEAR STITCH.

I had named the shop the Seven-Year Stitch for three reasons. One, it's an embroidery specialty shop. Two, I'm a huge fan of classic movies. And three, it actually took me seven years to turn my dream of owning an embroidery shop into a reality.

Once upon a time, in a funky-cool land called San Francisco, I was an accountant. Not a funky-cool job, believe me, especially for a funky-cool girl like me, Marcy Singer. I had a corner cubicle near a window. You'd think the window would be a good thing, but it looked out upon a vacant building that grew more dilapidated by the day. Maybe by the hour. It was majorly depressing. One year, a coworker gave me a cactus for my birthday. I set it in that window, and it died. I told you it was depressing.

Still, my job wasn't that bad. I can't say I truly enjoyed it, but I am good with numbers and the work was tolerable. Then I got the call from Sadie. Not *a* call, mind you; *the* call.

"Hey, Marce. Are you sitting down?" Sadie had said.

"Sadie, I'm always sitting down. I keep a stationary bike frame and pedal it under my desk so my leg muscles won't atrophy."

"Good. The hardware store next to me just went out of business."

"And this is good because you hate the hardware guy?"

She'd given me an exasperated huff. "No, silly. It's good because the space is for lease. I've already called the landlord, and he's giving you the opportunity to snatch it up before anyone else does."

Sadie is an entrepreneur. She and her husband, Blake, own MacKenzies' Mochas, a charming coffee shop on the Oregon coast. She thinks everyone — or, at least, Marcy Singer — should also own a charming shop on the Oregon coast.

"Wait, wait, wait," I'd said. "You expect me to come up there to Quaint City, Oregon —"

"Tallulah Falls, thank you very much."

"— and set up shop? Just like that?"

"Yes! It's not like you're happy there or like you're on some big five-year career plan."

"Thanks for reminding me."

"And you've not had a boyfriend or even a date for more than a year now. I could still strangle David when I think of how he broke your heart."

"Once again, thank you for the painful reminder."

"So what's keeping you there? This is your chance to open up the embroidery shop you used to talk about all the time in college."

"But what do I know about actually run-

9

ning a business?"

Sadie had huffed. "You can't tell me you've been keeping companies' books all these years without having picked up some pointers about how to — and how not to — run a business."

"You've got a point there. But what about Angus?"

"Marce, he will *love* it here! He can come to work with you every day, run up and down the beach. . . . Isn't that better than the situation he has now?"

I swallowed a lump of guilt the size of my fist.

"You're right, Sadie," I'd admitted. "A change will do us both good."

That had been three months ago. Now I was a resident of Tallulah Falls, Oregon, and today was the grand opening of the Seven-Year Stitch.

A cool, salty breeze off the ocean ruffled my hair as I hopped out of the bright red Jeep I'd bought to traipse up and down the coast.

Angus followed me out of the Jeep and trotted beside me up the river-rock steps to the walk that connected all the shops on this side of the street. The shops on the other side of the street were set up in a similar manner, with river-rock steps lead-

10

ing up to walks containing bits of shells and colorful rocks for aesthetic appeal. A narrow, two-lane road divided the shops, and black wrought-iron lampposts and benches added to the inviting community feel. A large clock tower sat in the middle of the town square, pulling everything together and somehow reminding us all of the preciousness of time. Tallulah Falls billed itself as the friendliest town on the Oregon coast, and so far, I had no reason to doubt that claim.

I unlocked the door and flipped the CLOSED sign to OPEN before turning to survey the shop. It was as if I were seeing it for the first time. And, in a way, I was. I'd been here until nearly midnight last night, putting the finishing touches on everything. This was my first look at the finished project. Like all my finished projects, I tried to view it objectively. But, like all my finished projects, I looked upon this one as a cherished child.

The floor was black-and-white tile, laid out like a gleaming chessboard. All my wood accents were maple. On the floor to my left, I had maple bins holding cross-stitch threads and yarns. When a customer first came in the door, she would see the cross-stitch threads. They started in white and went through shades of ecru, pink, red, orange, yellow, green, blue, purple, gray, and black. The yarns were organized the same way on the opposite side. Perle flosses, embroidery hoops, needles, and cross-stitch kits hung on maple-trimmed corkboard over the bins. On the other side of the corkboard — the side with the yarn — there were knitting needles, crochet hooks, tapestry needles, and needlepoint kits.

The walls were covered by shelves where I displayed pattern books, dolls with dresses I'd designed and embroidered, and framed samplers. I had some dolls for those who liked to sew and embroider outfits (like me), as well as for those who enjoy knitting and crocheting doll clothes.

Standing near the cash register was my life-size mannequin, who bore a striking resemblance to Marilyn Monroe, especially since I put a short, curly blond wig on her and did her makeup. I even gave her a mole . . . er, beauty mark. I called her Jill. I was going to name her after Marilyn's character in *The Seven Year Itch,* but she didn't have a name. Can you believe that — a main character with no name? She was simply billed as "The Girl."

To the right of the door was the sitting area. As much as I loved to play with the amazing materials displayed all over the store, the sitting area was my favorite place in the shop. Two navy overstuffed sofas faced each other across an oval maple coffee table. The table sat on a navy, red, and white braided rug. There were red club chairs with matching ottomans near either end of the coffee table, and candlewick pillows with lace borders scattered over both the sofas. I made those, too — the pillows, not the sofas.

The bell over the door jingled, and I turned to see Sadie walking in with a travel coffee mug.

I smiled. "Is that what I think it is?"

"It is, if you think it's a nonfat vanilla latte with a hint of cinnamon." She handed me the mug. "Welcome to the neighborhood."

"Thanks. You're the best." The steaming mug felt good in my hands. I looked back over the store. "It looks good, doesn't it?"

"It looks fantastic. You've outdone yourself." She cocked her head. "Is that what you're wearing tonight?"

Happily married for the past five years, Sadie was always eager to play matchmaker for me. I hid a smile and held the hem of my vintage tee as if it were a dress. "You don't think Snoopy's Joe Cool is appropriate for the grand opening party?"

Sadie closed her eyes.

"I have a supercute dress for tonight," I said with a laugh, "and Mr. O'Ruff will be sporting a black tie for the momentous event."

Angus wagged his tail at the sound of his surname.

"Marce, you and that *pony*." Sadie scratched Angus behind the ears.

"He's a proud boy. Aren't you, Angus?"

Angus barked his agreement, and Sadie chuckled.

"I'm proud, too . . . of both of you." She grinned. "I'd better get back over to Blake. I'll be back to check on you again in a while."

Though we're the same age and had been roommates in college, Sadie clucked over me like a mother hen. It was sweet, but I could do without the fix-ups. Some of these guys she'd tried to foist on me . . . I have no idea where she got them — mainly because I was afraid to ask.

I went over to the counter and placed my big yellow purse and floral tote bag on the bottom shelf before finally taking a sip of my latte.

"That's yummy, Angus. It's nice to have a friend who owns a coffee shop, isn't it?"

Angus lay down on the large bed I'd put

14

behind the counter for him.

"That's a good idea," I told him. "Rest up. We've got a big day and an even bigger night ahead of us."

At about ten a.m., a woman wearing a smart black pantsuit, a paisley scarf, and bold silver jewelry entered the shop. *My first customer.* I caught my breath when I saw that she was holding a list.

"Good morning," I said. "Welcome to the Seven-Year Stitch. I'm Marcy Singer. May I help you find anything?"

The woman smiled. "I'm working on a cross-stitch piece for my granddaughter, and I need some metallic threads, beads, and ribbon to finish it. Everything is written down here." She handed me the list.

I was relieved to see that I had in stock everything she needed. I invited her to take a look around the shop, or to take a seat in the sitting area while I gathered her items.

"I'm having an open house tonight, if you'd like to stop by," I said as I put skeins of metallic thread into a shopping basket. "It's just a drop-in event — nothing fancy."

"I'll try to stop by," she said. "This is really a lovely shop."

I couldn't help feeling a burst of pride. "Thanks. It certainly doesn't appear that

15

you need lessons yourself, but if you know anyone who'd be interested, I have sign-up sheets for crewel, cross-stitch, and candle-wick classes — beginning and advanced — on the counter."

"Oh, I've always wanted to learn to do crewel." She stood and walked to the counter. "I'll sign up for that one, and my friend Martha might be interested, as well."

"Terrific." I returned to the counter with all the items on her list.

"I'm Sarah Crenshaw, by the way."

"Sarah, it's a pleasure to meet you. You're my first customer, and as such, I'd like to offer you a ten-percent discount," I said in my best professional-shopkeeper voice.

Well, now I knew there was one sure way to put a smile on my customers' faces.

As she left, I called, "I hope to see you this evening."

"I'll see what I can do."

When she was out of sight, I dropped to the floor and hugged Angus. "Our cash register has actual cash in it!"

He wagged his tail.

The rest of the day passed quickly. Some Tallulah Falls residents stopped by to wish me well; many bought threads, patterns, and fabrics, and most promised to return for the evening's festivities. Sadie and Blake had enjoyed a busy day next door at MacKenzies' Mochas, too, but Sadie had still managed to stop in for a quick hello after the lunch rush.

I closed the shop and hurried home to get ready. I had an actual house here, as opposed to the apartment I had in San Francisco. I bought the house shortly after leasing the shop, and I had finally finished unpacking the past weekend. Of course, in San Fran, I spent a lot of time at Mom's house, too, which was okay, but that doesn't lend itself to a mature, independent lifestyle.

I liked being a homeowner. Sadie said it was because nothing had been broken yet, but I was optimistic. I'm not bragging, but my two-story house was gorgeous . . . especially compared to the cramped little apartment I had overlooking the San Francisco Bay. Here, while I didn't have a direct view of the ocean, I could hear it all the time. It was wonderfully serene. I was also within walking distance of the beach, which was great, because Angus seemed to adore romping along the shore.

I went upstairs to get ready. I showered, dried my hair, and then padded into the bedroom to get dressed. I opened the closet and took out my black lace dress. I slipped

17

the dress over my head and smoothed the material over my hips. The dress came to just above my knees, but it didn't do much to make me look taller. Maybe the four-inch-high red stilettos would help. The black did make my pale skin and platinum hair stand out, especially with my splash of red lipstick. I was going for an Old Hollywood look, and I thought I was pulling if off rather well.

My mind drifted back to Mom as I dug through my jewelry box for my pair of jet beaded chandelier earrings I love so much. You could say Angus and I had gone and loaded up the truck and moved to Beverly. But actually, we'd moved *away* from Beverly — Singer, that is, aka Mom, movie-costume designer extraordinaire.

I gave myself a mental shake. Why in the world was I thinking *The Beverly Hillbillies* theme song? Of course, thinking about *The Beverly Hillbillies* brought Buddy Ebsen to mind. And that, in turn, made me remember he'd played Audrey Hepburn's estranged husband in *Breakfast at Tiffany's.* Random trivia seems to be always lurking just beneath the surface of my mind.

I took a long black cigarette holder from inside my jewelry box and placed it between my teeth. Mom had given it to me years ago. It had been a prop on some movie set. God only knew who had used it, so she'd insisted on scalding it before giving it to me. Good thing. While I've never been a smoker, I used to love pretending to use the long black cigarette holder. It made me remember how even Lucille Ball as Lucy Ricardo had used one to make her look sophisticated after she and Ethel had attended charm school.

I sighed. Leaving Mom behind in San Francisco had been the one drawback to my moving to Tallulah Falls. I wished Mom could have made the party, but she was in New York on a movie set. It was par for the course. In many ways, I grew up privileged. But I was lonely for my mother, who was often on location somewhere, and since Dad had died when I was very young, I'd often been left in the care of my nanny.

I have to give Mom credit for passing along to me my love of textiles, though. When she was home, Mom often allowed me to come to the studio and help work with the fabrics. She'd wanted me to go into fashion and costume design. A rebellious little snot at the time, I'd told her I wanted a "more stable and reliable" career. Mom said I'd be bored with a reliable career. While I'd admitted that accounting wouldn't be as exciting as dressing Hollywood's A-listers, I asserted that it would allow me to be home for my family, should I ever be fortunate enough to have one. I told you I was a rebellious little snot. That comment had hurt Mom. And I'd meant it to. At the time, I wouldn't have taken it back for anything in the world, even if I could have. Now that I was a wee bit older and wiser, I regretted it.

During my rebellious late-teen years, I even stopped going to Mom's studio. It was like I was spiting her, but I was really hurting only myself. I hadn't realized that until I was in college. I'd come back to the dorm one evening to find Sadie laboriously trying to embroider a pair of jeans. I took over the task and rediscovered my love for the craft. Still, I was too proud to admit that to Mom, so I'd sucked it up and embarked on my career in accounting.

I found the chandelier earrings I'd been looking for and put them on. Taking one last imaginary puff from the cigarette holder, I placed it back in the jewelry box.

I called Angus to me and put his black bow tie around his neck. Then I batted my lashes at him and imitated Bette Davis: "Fasten your seat belts. It's going to be a bumpy night."

When Angus and I got to the shop, Sadie and Blake were already there setting up a refreshment buffet on the counter.

"We used the key you gave me," Sadie said. "I hope you don't mind."

"Why would I mind? I just wish I'd arrived earlier. You two already have all the work done." I inhaled deeply, savoring the chocolate-and-vanilla-scented air. "Everything looks — and smells — delicious."

"And you look beautiful," Blake said. "Todd will be thrilled."

"Blake!" Sadie frowned at her husband.

I looked from one to the other. "Who's Todd?"

Blake looked at Sadie. "You didn't tell her?"

"Tell me what?"

The pair continued conversing as if I hadn't spoken. That made me even more nervous than I already was.

"Of course I didn't tell her," Sadie said. "I didn't want her to think I was trying to fix her up."

"You mean you're not?"

Sadie sighed. "Not exactly. I wanted to introduce the two of them. That's all —

nothing more."

"Uh-huh." Blake grinned knowingly. "That's all, huh?"

Sadie swatted at him playfully with a paper plate, and he pulled her to him for a quick kiss.

They're a sweet couple . . . well suited, even though on the surface they appear so different. Sadie is tall and dark. Blake is only an inch or two taller than his wife, and stockily built with blue eyes and light blond hair. They're opposites in other ways, as well: Sadie hates sports, while Blake *loves* hockey; Sadie likes corny horror flicks, but Blake likes corny comedies; Sadie enjoys reading the classics, and Blake's reading seems to be confined to blogs — really dorky blogs, to be exact. And yet you can look at them and see how much they love each other, how compatible they truly are.

I hope to find a love like that myself one day. I thought I'd had it once, but I'd been so wrong. And, based on Sadie's previous attempts, I doubted I'd find it with this Todd guy. Or anyone else Sadie happened to dig out from under a rock.

"Blake is right about your looking beautiful," Sadie said. "Though I'll never know how you walk in those shoes."

"You'll never have to find out," I said.

"You're tall enough without them. And you look terrific, by the way."

Sadie looked down at her navy dress with the beaded bodice. "Aw, this old thing?" She winked as Blake rolled his eyes.

I went to take a closer look at the refreshments while Blake fed Angus a shortbread cookie. There was a carafe of hot chocolate and another of Kona coffee. I thought fleetingly of asking the MacKenzies about a pot of decaf, but decided not to. Let everyone eat, drink, and be wired.

Besides the aforementioned shortbread cookies, there were s'mores, chocolate chip cookies, and peanut butter crinkles. The napkins had THE SEVEN-YEAR STITCH superimposed over an image of Marilyn Monroe standing on a grate with her dress billowing about her thighs. Blake had found the napkins online somewhere. Blake could find *anything* online.

I turned back to my friends. "Thank you so much, guys. This means a lot to me."

Sadie smiled. "You're welcome. You mean a lot to us."

That's when I knew I'd have to give this Todd guy a chance . . . no matter what he might be like.

"Will you help me keep an eye on Angus tonight?" I asked. "You know he has no problem reaching the counter; and with everybody's attention diverted, he might just give in to temptation." I looked at Angus, who wagged his tail and looked up at me with a "Who me?" expression.

"Yeah, especially since Blake has already got him started on those shortbread cookies," Sadie said. "They're addictive. Trust me, I know."

"Sorry." Blake looked sheepish, but slipped another cookie behind his back to Angus.

The bell over the door heralded the first guest.

"Am I too early?"

Before I could turn to see who'd spoken, I was struck by the richness of his voice, smooth and delicious as warm maple syrup dripping off a hot pancake on an icy January morning. I turned, half expecting to be disappointed. I was not disappointed.

"You're right on time," I said, taking in the man's thick, dark hair and sparkling brown eyes. I held out my hand. "I'm Marcy Singer. Welcome to the Seven-Year Stitch."

From the corner of my eye, I noticed Sadie and Blake elbowing each other as the man encased my hand in his own.

"Nice to meet you, Marcy. I'm Todd Calloway."

Angus placed his big snout on our clasped hands to effectively end the handshake.

"Well, hey, big fellow," Todd said. "Do you embroider, or are you only here for the party?"

"He's here for the shortbread," Blake said.

To everyone's delight, Angus sat and offered Todd his large gray paw to shake.

Wow, I thought, *even Angus approves.* I caught Sadie's eye and gave her an appreciative smile. If she'd dug Todd Calloway out from under a rock, that rock must've been a diamond.

Before I really knew what was happening, the shop was full. Sadie and Blake introduced me to the people I hadn't met earlier in the day. Still, it was going to be hard to remember everyone.

I looked around the room and caught sight of Todd Calloway. He was bending over to hear what some short older woman with her hair in a supersevere bun was telling him. When he caught my eye, he raised his coffee cup in salute.

I grinned. There was at least one person here I'd have no trouble remembering.

I sought out Angus and spotted him sitting beside a lovely girl with honey-colored hair. The girl, who appeared to be in her early teens, was stroking Angus' head and speaking to him softly.

"Hi, I'm Marcy," I said, approaching the girl. I nodded at Angus. "Angus likes you."

"Thanks. I like him, too. People say I'm good with dogs."

"You sure are."

From the corner of my eye, I glimpsed a lanky, unkempt man wearing dirty jeans and a trucker cap coming toward us. He staggered into me and caused me to stumble. Angus stiffened as I caught the back of the red chair to steady myself.

"It's okay, Angus," I said softly.

"I needa talk with you," the man said.

"Okay," I said, my voice wavering a little.

The man was obviously drunk, and he was making me uneasy. I walked slowly away from Angus so the dog wouldn't sense my anxiety. The man followed with an unsteady gait.

"This used ta be my store," the man said.

"Oh, then you must be Mr. Enright," I said, having heard his name from both Sadie and my new landlord.

"Yep. Tim Enright. Thirty years, this was Enright's Hardware."

"It —" I cleared my throat. "It must be hard for you to see the place change hands. I —"

26

Mr. Enright shook his head. "No, not that. Something else. We needa talk."

I glanced around and was relieved to see Blake coming to my rescue.

"Hey, Tim! How're you doing?" He put his arm around Mr. Enright's shoulders and propelled him away from me.

"I needa talk to her," Mr. Enright said. "Gotta tell her."

"Aw, that can wait, man. Come on over and check out the refreshments."

Mr. Enright tried to turn back to me, but Blake had a firm grip and led him over to the counter.

I had no idea why Mr. Enright would want to talk with me. I was giving that some thought when Sadie came over with a slender woman with light gray hair and small, round glasses. The woman wore a white, knee-length tunic and scarf over matching pants.

"Marcy, I'd like you to meet Rajani Singh."

"Please, call me Reggie," the woman said. "Everyone does."

"It's nice to meet you, Reggie," I said, holding out my hand.

She shook it. "Likewise. I love to embroider" — she held out the end of her scarf to reveal intricately embroidered white orchids

27

— "so I know you and I will get on swimmingly."

"I'm sure we will." I took a closer look at her scarf. "This is chikankari, isn't it?" Chikankari is a traditional form of white-on-white embroidery from India. "You do lovely work."

"Thank you." A grin spread across her face — Reggie seemed pleased that I recognized her form of embroidery.

"Reggie is the local librarian," Sadie said.

"Then I'm sure we'll see a lot of each other," I said with a laugh. "I love to read. And I love looking through art books for embroidery ideas."

"I do, too," Reggie said. "I wish my husband could've been here tonight, but he's on duty. He's on the police force."

"That must be an exciting job," I said.

"It has its moments, I guess. Manu loves it, but the hours can be a pain."

"Speaking of being a pain, what's with Tim Enright this evening?" Sadie asked. "He looks horrible."

"This is the first time I've ever met him," I said. I bit my lower lip. "Does he drink a lot?"

Reggie shook her head. "I've known Timothy for more than twenty years, and I've never known him to take a drink."

Before either Sadie or I could respond, a heavyset woman with short, curly brown hair interrupted. She wore a severe gray suit and pumps. The suit seemed to belie the woman's outgoing personality.

"Excuse me," she said. "I'm Vera Langhorne. I have to run, but I didn't want to leave before meeting the guest of honor." She shook my hand warmly.

"Thank you so much for coming tonight, Mrs. Langhorne," I said. "I hope you'll come back when we have more time to visit."

"Oh, I will. I've signed up for one of your classes. I'm looking forward to it."

"So am I," I said.

As Mrs. Langhorne walked away, Timothy Enright approached me and took me by the arm. "Come 'ere. Gotta tell you."

"Please, Mr. Enright," I began. "I'm sorry I —"

"Tim!" It was Todd Calloway. "How've you been?" He widened his eyes at me and led Tim Enright away.

Mr. Enright turned back to me, his eyes pleading. I'd have felt sorry for him if I weren't so freaked-out by his behavior. Since I *was* freaked-out, I took the opportunity to walk away and lose myself in the crowd.

■ ■ ■ ■

Two hours later, everyone except Sadie, Blake, Todd, Angus, and I had gone. I slipped off my shoes and padded around in my stocking feet while helping Blake and Sadie clean up.

"Ms. Singer," Todd said, "I believe your open house was a rousing success."

"Thank you. I do, too. Look at how many people signed up for embroidery classes."

Sadie looked over my shoulder at the lists. "Impressive."

Suddenly, we heard a thud. It appeared to have come from the back of the building.

"What was that?" I asked.

"Probably just a dog turning over a trash can," Blake said.

"We get that a lot," Sadie said. "If you throw any food in the garbage cans out back, be sure to double bag it."

"Or even triple bag it," Todd said. "Because of the bears."

"Bears?"

"Oh, sure. They come scrounging around every now and then." He caught Blake's eye and grinned. "In fact, I should probably walk you out to your car just in case that *was* a bear."

The next morning, it became clear that a bear had not caused the thud we'd heard.

CHAPTER TWO

I was feeling good as Angus and I unlocked the door and entered the shop the next morning. I had my lists in hand and was eager to start calling people about the first embroidery classes. About seven people had signed up for the cross-stitch tote bag project. Twice as many had signed up for beginner's crewel and candlewick classes. Besides that, many of the women at the party had indicated an interest in stopping by for "Sit and Stitch" sessions between eleven a.m. and one p.m. every Tuesday, Wednesday, and Thursday.

Suddenly, Angus ran to the storeroom and began pawing the door.

"What's up with you? You're usually not this active until you've been awake at least an hour or two." I strode to the storeroom and flung open the door. "There. Now are you —"

I screamed. Timothy Enright was lying on

the storeroom floor. Unfortunately, the sight failed to pull Angus up short. He ran forward to sniff Mr. Enright.

"Angus, no!" I grabbed his collar, wrestled the huge beast out of the storeroom, and closed the door. It was all I could do to pull him into the bathroom and shut him inside.

I leaned against the bathroom door and tried to catch my breath. My body was shaking so hard, and I was afraid I was going to be sick. Or faint. Or both. I'm usually not a fainter, but I don't have the strongest stomach in the world, and it didn't smell great inside the storeroom.

Poor Mr. Enright. Had he passed out and been on that cold concrete floor all night long? I knew I had to pull myself together long enough to go back and see about him.

I went back to the storeroom and eased open the door. I half expected him to jump up off the floor to let me know this whole thing had been a prank. But he didn't move.

I covered my mouth and nose with the sleeve of my sweater in an attempt to escape the sickening smell.

Mr. Enright's trucker cap had been knocked off when he'd fallen, and I could see he had a sparse patch of brown hair covering his head. He'd thrown a few of the boxes off the storeroom shelves, and every

OCD impulse I've ever had surfaced in a ridiculous desire to put my once-tidy storeroom back in order. That pale rose cloth with the dainty floral pattern shouldn't be lying on the floor. Nor should those wooden embroidery hoops. They're delicate. If someone stepped on them, they'd break. And those tapestry needles . . . while not terribly sharp, someone could get hurt if they weren't picked up and put back in their box.

I closed my eyes and realized the futility of my desire to restore order to this situation before even calling the paramedics. First things first. I needed to get Mr. Enright some medical attention.

"Mr. Enright, are you okay?" My voice was muffled thanks to the sweater, but I simply could not stand to smell that air. In his drunken state, Mr. Enright must have thrown up. "Can you get up, sir?" I bent lower to see if he was trying to speak. He wasn't, but I noticed he had one of the tapestry needles in his right hand. I glanced at the wall in front of him and saw that he'd scratched the words *four square fifth w* into the light blue paint.

"Mr. Enright!" I called again. Since he showed no signs of reviving, I went to the counter and called the ambulance. Angus barked his protests from behind the bathroom door.

With reassurance that the paramedics were on their way, I hung up the phone and went to wait by the front window.

Within just a few minutes, I heard sirens blaring down the road. I hurried and opened the door wide.

"He's in the storeroom," I told the paramedics as they rolled a stretcher quickly through the door. "All the way in the back."

Before the paramedics reached the storeroom, Sadie came barreling into the shop. "Marcy!" she called, her eyes darting all around the front room.

"I'm here." I hurried to greet her.

"Are you okay?" Sadie asked. "I saw the ambulance stop outside."

"I'm fine, Sadie. But . . . Mr. Enright's not. He passed out on my storeroom floor last night."

Sadie rolled her eyes. "Man. Did he throw up or anything?"

I grimaced. "It's not pretty in there."

"Ewww!" Sadie began fanning her face with one hand and took her cell phone from her jacket pocket with the other. "I'll call Blake and have him look up the phone number for one of those hazmat cleaning teams the very first chance he gets."

"Hazmat?"

"Hazardous materials? You don't want to be cleaning up that storeroom yourself."

"Ugh. You've got a point."

Sadie dialed Blake and turned around as she quietly explained the situation.

A burly paramedic strode out of the storeroom. "Miss, I need you to lock the front door. We need to secure the area until the police arrive."

"The police?" I asked. "But I don't want to press charges. Mr. Enright must've staggered in there during the party last night and passed out — that's all. I don't think he broke in this morning before I got here or anything like that." I peered at him. "Do you?"

"I'm not at liberty to comment, miss. Please lock the door until the police arrive." With that, he abruptly went back to the storeroom and closed the door.

I locked the front door and flipped the CLOSED sign over as Sadie returned her cell phone to her pocket.

"What the heck was his problem?"

"I don't know," I said. "But apparently, the paramedics have called the police and they're on their way."

"You don't . . ." Sadie's voice trailed away.

"I don't what?"

"You don't think he's . . . dead. Do you?"

"D-dead? Why would he be dead?" My voice had become a shrill shriek. Probably whales were hearing me miles offshore.

"I don't know. Maybe when he fell, he hit his head on something."

"Like what, for goodness sake? A bag of pillow stuffing?"

"It'll be okay," Sadie said unconvincingly. "The police will be here in a few minutes, and we'll get everything sorted out." She tried to smile, but her lips were quivering too badly to pull it off.

She was partially right. The police did arrive quickly; but, unfortunately, nothing was sorted out. With Angus still barking furiously from the bathroom, Sadie and I were told to wait in the sitting area and not to move around the shop until we could speak with the detective in charge. A uniformed patrolman stayed to keep us company, or, rather, to babysit us.

"What's going on?" I asked.

The patrolman, a young Native American, most likely from the local Clatsop tribe, simply stood with his feet shoulder width apart and his hands clasped behind his back.

"Please!" I said. "This is my store. I have a right to know what's going on!"

He looked down at me with gentle brown

eyes. "I'm sorry. You'll have to wait."

Finally, a tall, lean, clean-shaven man, young but with salt-and-pepper hair, emerged from the storeroom. "Ms. Singer . . . Mrs. MacKenzie." He nodded to each of us in turn. To me he said, "I'm Ted Nash, chief detective for the Tallulah Falls Police Department. I need to speak with you ladies separately."

"What's going on, Ted?" Sadie asked.

The detective hesitated a moment and then admitted, "Timothy Enright is dead."

"How?" Sadie asked. "Did he hit his head on something when he fell, or —"

"Sadie . . . Mrs. MacKenzie, I can't talk to you and Ms. Singer together. Go on next door, and I'll be there when I'm finished here."

Sadie stood. "She had nothing to do with this. We —"

"Mrs. MacKenzie, do I need to have you escorted next door?"

Sadie huffed. "No, Ted, you do not need to have me escorted anywhere. I'm going."

"Thank you."

I stood, showed the key to the detective, and — upon his nod — unlocked the door for Sadie.

"I'll talk to you as soon as he leaves," Sadie whispered.

I merely nodded and locked the door behind her. I returned to the sitting area. The detective gestured for me to sit on the sofa.

I said nothing. I merely sat and stared at the tweed pattern on his sport jacket. I resented his treating me as if I'd done something wrong.

"Do you have any idea why Mr. Enright was in your storeroom?"

"No. I suppose he might've wandered in there by mistake." I shrugged. "We . . . There was an open house here last night. Mr. Enright came and kept wanting to tell me something."

"What did he tell you?"

"Not a thing. He appeared to be drunk, and I avoided him as much as possible."

Detective Nash wrote in his notebook before leveling his gaze back at me. "Was liquor served at this party?"

"No. The MacKenzies took care of the refreshments. We had hot cocoa, coffee, and assorted cookies."

"What made you think Timothy Enright was inebriated?"

"Well, he was staggering . . . slurring his words."

"I see." Again, the detective wrote in his notebook.

I glanced up at the patrolman. He was looking straight ahead, as stoic as a Buckingham Palace guard. I turned my attention back to the detective.

"So, what happened to him?"

"We don't know, Ms. Singer. Our forensics team is on its way, and we should know more after they and the coroner complete their investigations."

"In the meantime, I need to stay out of the storeroom, right?"

The detective looked sharply up from his notes. "In the meantime, you need to stay out of this store. It's to remain closed until the crime-scene investigators are finished and —"

"Crime-scene investigators? Since when is this a crime scene?"

Ted Nash focused his level gaze on me. "This became a crime scene when a man died on your property."

A baker's dozen more questions and a few hours later, I was back in my living room, sitting to the right of the fireplace in a white suede chair, talking on my cell phone. I'd been calling people who'd enrolled in my classes all afternoon to let them know the store would be closed for the next few days. I could see Sadie coming up the walk. She waved to me, and I motioned her inside.

Angus met Sadie at the door. Despite Sadie's calling Angus a pony and scolding Blake for spoiling him, she had a soft spot for the dog. She dropped to her knees there in the foyer, took his head in her hands, and crooned to him softly.

"I know you were scared in that old bathroom today. Yes, you were. And Marcy and I were a little scared ourselves." She kissed the top of Angus' head.

I had turned off the phone and walked to the foyer. Hearing Sadie's testament to being a little scared, I admitted, "Marcy is still scared."

"I know." Sadie stood and hugged me. "Sadie is still a little shaken up herself."

Grinning at our silliness, I asked, "Did Blake call the hazmat guys for me?"

"Yeah. They said they'll coordinate with the forensics guys and start cleaning as soon as they can. They've already come by the coffee shop and gotten the key. So they're working on it."

"Thank you. That's good to know. I've been telling people I'll open back up as soon as I can. I was hoping we'd have the first embroidery class tomorrow evening, as scheduled. But . . ."

"Yeah, I don't know about that. I'm not

sure the police and the cleaning crew will be finished by then. Of course, you could always hold class here. Did anybody back out?" Sadie asked.

"No, but everybody wanted to hear all about Mr. Enright."

"What did you tell them?"

I motioned for Sadie to join me in the kitchen. "I've been telling them I found him in the storeroom and that it appears he suffered some sort of accident." I opened the refrigerator. Focusing on mundane activities helped settled my nerves. "Want some juice?"

"What've you got?"

"Orange, mango, tomato."

"Tomato, please."

I poured two small glasses of tomato juice, and Sadie and I sat down at the table.

"What did Nash say to you?" I asked.

"Not much. He asked if anyone else at the party got sick."

I uttered a growl of frustration. "Enright wasn't sick. He was drunk."

"That's what I said. But Ted insists Tim Enright was a lifelong teetotaler."

"So? There's a first time for everything."

"True," Sadie said. "And from what I've been hearing around the coffee shop, the guy was going through a lot." She took a sip of her juice. "He lost his business, his wife, Lorraine. . . ."

"Then why does Ted Nash have such a hard time believing the poor man decided to partake of a little fruit of the vine?"

"I don't know. But he apparently found it more plausible that Blake and I spiked the coffee."

I shook my head. "What galls me is that what happened is obvious to everyone except the detective investigating the case."

"Did he ask you about the message Enright scratched on the wall with one of your tapestry needles?"

"That *four square fifth w* weirdness? Yeah, he mentioned it. To me, it's further proof of Enright's drunkenness."

"Still, you have to wonder what he meant by it," Sadie said. "I mean, he was apparently still scratching on that wall when he died."

"Probably because there was nobody there to help him." I dropped my chin. "I feel horrible about that. I should've checked the storeroom before I left last night."

Sadie took my hand. "You didn't know. None of us did. And, well, we thought we were the last to leave."

I sniffled. "If I'd checked that stupid storeroom last night, Mr. Enright might be alive today."

"Sweetie, please stop beating yourself up. What happened couldn't be helped. And if Ted is right and Tim Enright was poisoned —"

My head shot up. "Nash thinks Enright was poisoned? He didn't tell me that."

"Probably because Blake and I served the food. He needed to know if anyone else got sick or acted strangely."

"So if he was poisoned . . ."

Sadie nodded. "Then he was likely poisoned before he showed up at your party."

There was a pounding at the front door, followed immediately by Angus' bark.

"Hey, hey," came Blake's voice from the foyer. "It's only your friendly neighborhood caterers."

"In that case, we're in the kitchen," Sadie called.

Blake and Todd came into the kitchen with Angus on their heels.

"I hope you don't mind my tagging along with Blake," Todd said to me. "I heard about all the hoopla going on at your shop and wanted to come by to see if there's any way I can help."

"Thanks, Todd, but I'm not sure what anyone can do at this point."

"I know what we can do," Blake said, set-

44

ting two large, insulated bags on the table. "We can eat." He took a platter of chicken salad on croissants from one of the bags.

I smiled. "My favorite." Blake made his own chicken salad from all white meat and pecans and white seedless grapes. It was delicious.

"I know it." Waggling his eyebrows at Sadie, Blake took out the next platter. It was an array of fruit with a cream-cheese dip in the middle.

"And that's *my* favorite," Sadie said. "Thoughtfulness. It's why I married that man."

Blake feigned hurt. "I thought it was my great butt."

"I don't like you for your thoughtfulness or your butt," Todd said. "Now haul out those brownies."

Relieved at how the men had lightened the mood, I retrieved plates, glasses, and silverware. "What do you do, Todd? In all the excitement last night, I forgot to ask."

Todd lifted a six-pack of bottles from the other insulated bag. "This is what I do."

I cocked my head. "You drink beer?"

"Well, yes." Todd chuckled. "But I own a craft brewery and pub. It's just across the street from your shop, as a matter of fact."

"The Brew Crew?"

"That's me. My mom wanted me to call the place Hot Toddy's, but I flatly refused."

I laughed, but I had to silently agree that Mr. Calloway was one hot Toddy.

"What flavor did you bring?" Sadie asked.

"Apricot ale. I figured it would complement both the chicken salad and the fruit, and then we can have coffee with the brownies."

"Wow," I said, "you guys thought of everything."

We filled our plates, and then Sadie, Blake, and Todd watched as I tried my first sip of apricot ale. I raised my glass to my lips, my eyes searching each of their faces, particularly Sadie's, for a clue as to what this golden concoction might taste like. It smelled fruity, but I'm not a big beer drinker, and fruity scent aside, this was beer. Still, I didn't want to hurt Todd's feelings. He'd made it himself.

Trying to take a deep breath and hold it without being too obvious, I took the teeniest of sips. It was good. It was actually good. It had a sweet, malty flavor, but was rather dry, like wine. I took another drink.

"I think she likes it," Sadie said.

"I do. It's not what I was expecting. The apricot flavor is there, but I can also taste a hint of spice."

"It's a specialty yeast I use for brewing this flavor, among others," Todd said. "I'm glad you like the beer."

We enjoyed our meal. Even Angus had a chicken-salad sandwich, although he'd already had his supper before Sadie arrived. Blake offered to take Angus for a walk; but shortly after he disappeared through the front door with a delighted Angus on a leash, he reappeared in the kitchen.

"Uh, Marcy," he said, looking worried, "Tim Enright's widow is here to see you. Lorraine. She won't say why she's here, but if you want, I can . . ."

I stood up, admittedly a little at a loss. "No, Blake, it's ok. I'll talk to her."

We all traipsed through to the foyer.

Standing right outside the door was a gaunt, red-haired woman.

"Lorraine?" I ventured.

"I take it you're Marcy Singer," the woman said. "I came to thank you for taking away not only Timothy's business, but his life, as well."

"What?" I asked, stepping to the forefront of the group. "How can you possibly think I had anything to do with Mr. Enright's business or his death? I only met your husband yesterday."

"You might've met Timothy only yester-

47

day," the woman said, "but I'm his wife, and I know for certain that if it wasn't for you and your artsy shop, Mr. Trelawney wouldn't have run Timothy out of business."

"That's ridiculous. I didn't even know the shop was available until Sadie called me in California after Mr. Enright had vacated it."

"That's right," Sadie said. "I didn't call her until I saw the For Lease sign in the window." Clearly, Mrs. Enright wasn't being totally logical. Sadie tried to calm her down. "I know this must be tough, Lorraine, to lose Tim even though you were divorcing."

"It wasn't final yet," Mrs. Enright said angrily. "I still have a stake in Timothy's financial affairs." Her tone obviously rubbed Angus the wrong way, and he gave one of his deep, resounding barks. Mrs. Enright started.

I could sense Angus getting tense and asked Blake to take him outside.

"So what are you more concerned with here, Mrs. Enright?" Todd asked. "What happened to your husband or his financial status?"

Mrs. Enright glared at him. "Timothy was my husband for twenty-five years. Of course

I'm concerned about what happened to him." She turned her baleful gaze on me. "As a matter of fact, I'll be talking with my attorney tomorrow morning to see if I have grounds to file a wrongful-death suit against you. And if I do, I'll see you in court, Ms. Singer."

With that, she turned and stormed out, leaving my guests and me dumbfounded.

CHAPTER THREE

Sadie and Blake left together after making sure I wasn't too shaken up by the Lorraine Enright incident. I was, but apparently I did a good job of hiding it. Todd stayed behind to help me "clean up."

"There's really not much to clean up, Todd," I said, loading our plates, glasses, cups, and silverware into the dishwasher.

"I know," he said, "but you have to admit, it was a gallant excuse to stay behind."

I smiled. "It was awfully gallant."

"I don't think Lorraine will be back tonight," he said, "but I'd like to hang around a while just to make sure."

"You don't have to do that. But I am glad you're here. And not just because of Lorraine. You want to go hang out in the living room?"

"After you."

We sat on the sofa near the fireplace. His dark jeans and black shirt were a stark contrast to my white suede sofa, but he looked great — handsome, comfortable, at ease with himself and his surroundings. I was glad I'd finished all my unpacking and that I'd finally gotten the house in order. I took off my shoes and slipped them under the cherry coffee table in front of the sofa.

"Have you lived in Tallulah Falls all your life?" I asked.

"Pretty much. I grew up here, went to college in Portland, and then came back here afterward."

"Gee, I'll bet you loved CliffsNotes in college," I teased. "I know your life has been more exciting than that. Can you give me the less-abbreviated version?"

"I did love CliffsNotes in college. Couldn't have passed high school English without them, either." He chuckled. "You, on the other hand, probably loved laboring over all those boring old texts."

"They're called *classics,* not boring old texts. And, yes, I did. I thought they were romantic. What was your favorite subject in school, since it so obviously wasn't literature?"

"Chemistry. It's how I got started in the beer business, actually. Dad was afraid I'd blow up the garage, so my senior year of high school, he began steering me toward

51

the craft brewery business."

"But isn't beer just as combustible as a lot of other things?" I asked.

"I guess it could be, but I think Dad figured other things didn't taste as good."

We both laughed.

"Do your mom and dad live nearby?"

"Yeah. Sometimes I feel it's too close, but usually I'm pretty happy to have them around. How about you? Miss your parents?"

"My mom," I said. Thinking of her gave me a twinge. At some point, I'd have to tell her about finding Timothy Enright's body. She wasn't going to like it. "I do miss her. I think it was time for me to spread my wings a little, though . . . take a flight a little farther from the nest."

Todd grinned. "If I had a beer, I'd drink to that."

After Todd left, I went upstairs to the master suite. I put on some soft music, took a warm bath, donned my favorite flannel pajamas, and confronted the inevitable. I called Mom.

I'd propped my pillows up against the headboard of my bed and slid under the covers, so I'd settled in for a long conversation. I was hoping to be able to pretend this was no big deal. I didn't want Mom to come rushing all the way across the country from her film location in upstate New York to my rescue. She'd done that a little too often in the past. It was time for me to stand on my own two feet. . . . Although, in a way, it would've been nice to have Mom there to lean on.

She answered on the first ring.

"Hi, Mom. It's me."

"Hello, darling! How is everything? I'm so sorry I missed your party last night. It must have been wonderful fun."

"It . . . it was. Everybody was really supportive and seemed to be excited about the shop."

"Fantastic."

"Yeah."

"That was a loaded *yeah* if I've ever heard one," she said. "What's going on?"

"There was a man at the party last night who was drunk. And this morning, Angus and I found him in the storeroom."

"He'd passed out in your storeroom?"

"Um . . . I guess you could say that," I hedged. "He . . . um . . . he —"

"Marcella?" She'd taken on that stern tone she'd always used when I was in trouble as a little girl.

"He died," I said. I blinked furiously, daring myself to cry.

"He *died?*"

"Yeah . . . he was . . . he was dead when Angus and I found him."

"Oh, darling. Do you need me to come out?"

"No, Mom, I'm fine. Really. I just had to close the shop for a few days until the cleaning crew can get the stockroom back in order."

"Well, if you need me, you know I'll hop on the next plane out," she said.

"I know, but really, everything is fine. Just a minor aggravation, more or less."

She sighed. "Still, finding that man in your storeroom must've scared you silly. I'm sorry this had to happen. Leave it to some drunken buffoon to wander in and not only spoil your party, but make you have to shut down your store to boot. What a shame."

"Yeah . . . what a shame."

We made small talk for a few more minutes before signing off. I heard Angus' toenails clicking on the hardwood floor outside my room.

"Come on, Angus," I said.

Tail wagging, he obliged, jumping up onto the bed. I stroked his fur, happy for the company. Mom had been put out about Timothy Enright's spoiling my party and store opening, but my mind kept going back to the fact that he was there to tell me something. Something important. And if the authorities were correct and he had been poisoned, it might've been something that cost Mr. Enright his life.

I spent most of the next day in a state of anxious listlessness. I fielded calls, answered questions, but mostly tried to keep a low profile.

After Mrs. Enright's scathing accusations, I wanted to talk with my landlord, Mr. Trelawney, to see just what had happened to cause Timothy Enright to close his business.

I called Mr. Trelawney's number, and his wife answered.

"Hello, Mrs. Trelawney. This is Marcy Singer."

"Oh, hello, dear. I'm glad you called. Are you enjoying your shop? I so wanted to come to your little party the other evening, but I was a bit under the weather. Allergies, I suppose. But I do hope you had a nice time."

It was really strange that she didn't appear to know about the murder. "Um . . . yes. Is . . . is Mr. Trelawney there? I have a question for him."

"Oh, certainly. He's just now finishing up his dinner. You take care, dear, and I'll be in to see you soon. Now, let me get Bill."

I really wondered why Mrs. Trelawney hadn't said anything about Timothy Enright. Could there possibly be someone in town who hadn't heard of the man's fatal visit to my storeroom?

Bill Trelawney came on the line. "Hello, Marcy. How are you, dear?"

"I'm fine, Mr. Trelawney. And I hope you are."

"Yes, I —"

"I'm calling to ask you about Timothy Enright."

"I heard his behavior was deplorable at your reception, and I'm sorry about that."

"Um . . . thank you. Did . . . did you not hear about . . . about my finding him in the storeroom?"

"Oh, now, that is truly unacceptable. I made it clear to Mr. Enright that he was not to disturb you in any way. All of his belongings should have been moved out of that shop long before you arrived."

"Mr. Trelawney, I don't think you understand. When I found Mr. Enright in the storeroom, he was dead."

"Are you quite sure?"

"Quite."

"Oh, my." There was a long pause. "That's another matter altogether, isn't it?"

"I'm afraid so. It's very upsetting. The death."

"Yes, yes," he said. "A real shock."

"I wanted to ask . . . It's not necessarily relevant, but I just have to know. . . . Mrs. Enright came by my house yesterday evening and accused me of putting her husband out of business."

"Now, we both know that's nonsense. Don't allow Lorraine Enright to befuddle you. I imagine she's terribly distraught."

"I realize that, of course. Even though she and Mr. Enright were going through a divorce —"

"Were they?"

"That's my understanding." I was getting frustrated with the entire conversation, so I decided to say something off-the-wall myself. "Say, does the phrase *four square fifth* mean anything to you?"

Mr. Trelawney got so quiet, I was afraid we'd been disconnected. "Mr. Trelawney?"

"Where did you hear that?" he asked softly.

"Mr. Enright wrote it on the storeroom wall before he died."

"He shouldn't have done that. Did he write anything else?"

"I believe he meant to. There was a *w* following *fifth.*"

"Can I come over to look at it?"

"Sure, but not until tomorrow. The police closed my shop while they investigated, and then a cleaning crew is supposed to be coming in."

"The police?"

"Yes."

"That's disturbing," he mumbled.

"Um . . . yes, it was. Finding Mr. Enright dead in the storeroom was very disturbing, also."

"I'll be there tomorrow morning, then."

"Okay, any—" I realized Mr. Trelawney had hung up. I wondered why the phrase had brought about such a reaction from him. I also wondered why neither he nor his wife seemed to know about Timothy Enright's death. The rest of the town certainly was abuzz over it.

When I arrived at the Seven-Year Stitch the next morning, I was relieved to see that everything looked tidy and clean. The hazmat cleaners had assured me they'd put the shop back in order, but I wasn't convinced until I'd seen it for myself. The samplers and dolls were on their shelves, Jill was at the register, the yarns and threads were in their proper order, and the furniture looked freshly vacuumed. Of course, this wasn't the area I'd been most concerned with.

After depositing Angus in the bathroom with the promise "It's only for a couple minutes," I timidly went to check the storeroom. It looked great. The hazmat team had done a wonderful job. The fabrics had been neatly returned to their boxes, the tapestry needles had been gathered and re-boxed, and the foul odor was gone. If not for the words still scratched in the wall, no one would ever suspect what had transpired here night before last.

I bent down to take a closer look at the odd inscription.

Four square fifth w.

"Four square fifth *what?*" I wondered. "Fifth *wheel?*" The scribbles were probably merely a reflection of Mr. Enright's confused state of mind.

Staying true to my word, I firmly closed the storeroom door and went to let Angus out of the bathroom. He bounded over to the storeroom door, sniffed, and then came to lie on his bed under the counter and chew on a toy.

I smiled at this further reassurance that the storeroom had been thoroughly cleaned.

Sadie dropped in about ten a.m. with coffee for both of us. I got up from behind the counter, and Sadie and I went over to the sitting area. Sadie chose to stretch out on one of the navy sofas, while I ensconced myself in one of the red chairs.

"Have you heard any more from Lorraine?" Sadie asked.

"Not yet. I did speak with my lawyer yesterday — actually, Mom's lawyer — and he said I have nothing to fear from a wrongful-death suit since I in no way contributed to Mr. Enright's death."

"That's a relief."

"Yeah. I still hope she doesn't file suit, though. I can do without the expense, not to mention more bad publicity."

Angus came over to my chair and whined.

"Sadie, can you watch the shop for a sec while I take him outside? Normally, it's no big deal, but I'm expecting Mr. Trelawney sometime today."

"Okay. This is our slow time, anyway."

"Thanks." I grabbed Angus' leash, and he hurried over to let me snap it onto his collar. "We'll hurry."

"No problem," Sadie said.

I took Angus out onto the street and headed in the direction of the clock tower. It was a grassy area with black wrought-iron benches and large wooden flower barrels. The barrels currently contained mums in shades of white, yellow, and pink.

Before we could get to the clock tower, a woman burst out of the aromatherapy shop. She was thin, had gunmetal gray hair, and was wearing red, thick-framed glasses.

"Hey," she said. "Aren't you Marcy Singer? Didn't you open that new shop down the street, the Seven-Year Stitch?"

I smiled. "Yes, as a matter of fact, I did. Do you like to embroider?"

"No, no," she said quickly. "I just wanted to ask you about Timothy Enright. I heard he died in your shop."

"Um, yes. That's right."

"Well, what happened?"

I shrugged. "Nobody really knows at this point."

"I saw that cleaning crew come in there with their white suits and hoods on and everything," she said. "What was that all about? Did Mr. Enright make some sort of mess?"

"I . . . I'm not at liberty to say, Ms. . . ."

Without giving me her name, she hurried on. "I knew Mr. Enright when he leased the shop, you know. He appeared to be a very nice man — never did anything untoward, as far as I know." She narrowed her eyes.

"So, what do you think made him snap?"

"I have no idea," I said. "Please excuse me. I need to walk Angus and then get back to my shop."

I hurried on to the clock tower. Angus fulfilled his obligations, I cleaned it up, and then we returned to the Seven-Year Stitch.

Sadie zeroed in on my face when I returned. "What happened?"

I removed Angus' leash. "The lady from the aromatherapy shop came out and wanted to know what happened to Timothy Enright."

"Oh, don't mind her. She makes it her hobby to butt into everyone else's businesses."

"She didn't strike me as a particularly nice person," I said, "which is too bad, because I like aromatherapy products."

"That's okay," Sadie said with small smile. "I know a wonderful place in Lincoln City that sells top-of-the-line stuff."

"Did Mr. Trelawney stop by?" I asked.

"Yeah, as a matter of fact, he did. He was all freaked about that writing on the wall in the storeroom. He wants it painted over as soon as possible and said he'll send someone over to look at it."

I rolled my eyes. "It's not that big a deal. Not as big a deal as it will be to have to move everything so the storeroom can be painted." I sighed. "Is that all he said?"

Sadie nodded. "He was in and out of here in less than five minutes. Totally out of character. He usually loves to talk."

"I thought it was weird that neither he nor Mrs. Trelawney knew about Timothy Enright's death."

"They don't get out as much as they used to. Maybe they're out of the loop these days."

"Maybe. But Mr. Trelawney knew Timothy Enright had behaved badly during the party. How could he know about that but not know about Mr. Enright's death?"

I closed up the shop at five p.m. and placed a sign in the window that I'd be back at seven. I desperately needed a respite from the stress of the past few days, so I took Angus down to the beach so we could walk along the shore. I unhooked the dog's leash to allow him to run on ahead and play while I strolled. The rhythmic crash of the waves was soothing. I smiled at a black oystercatcher as it waddled to a tide pool and dug in its orange bill to scrounge for food. Angus turned and ran back for a hug from me before scampering down the beach again. He's such a good dog.

Back when I worked at the accounting firm, Pat, one of our clients, had been fined and ordered to get rid of some of her dogs or face jail time. I'd heard that Pat was a dog breeder and that she sold Yorkshire terriers. I wanted a little female Yorkie I could name Dahlia and adorn with pink hair bows.

Our boss, Mr. Ely, had sent a few of us over to see what we could do to help. When we arrived at Pat's palatial home, I was impressed. The place was gorgeous. Surely her kennels must rival those of the Westminster Kennel Club. Pat took us out back, where the true state of the kennels broke my heart. Her operation was little more than a puppy mill.

One scruffy gray puppy cowered in a tiny cage by himself. He was not a Yorkie; he was actually an Irish wolfhound. But he needed me.

"It's all right," I'd cooed softly, my eyes filling with tears. I reached into the cage and pulled him out, cuddling him to me. "I'll take you with me and give you a great home." The very thought literally warmed my heart, or so I thought, until I realized the puppy had peed all over me.

I did have the best of intentions when I took him home. And I adored this puppy I'd dubbed Sir Angus O'Ruff. But I'd gotten him a year ago — not long after the boyfriend bust-up — and he'd pretty much outgrown my small apartment. Sadie had been right when she'd said the move here would do him good. I was hoping it would do me good, too.

I'd thought David — the boyfriend — and I would be married and on our way to happily ever after by now. Too bad he was a commitment-phobe . . . and *really* too bad he didn't realize that before the dress was bought, the invitations were sent, and the church was booked. Mom still thought I was moving to Oregon to escape the embarrassment. I kept telling her I was over it, but I have to admit, the thought of getting out of the same state where David and our mutual, pitying friends lived was a comfort.

"Marcy!"

I turned to see a woman wearing jeans rolled to the knees. She was still too far away for me to recognize, so I started walking to meet the woman halfway.

"I don't want to disturb your walk," the woman said. "I just want to make sure we're still on for class this evening."

When I got closer to the woman, I could see it was Vera Langhorne. I smiled. "Yes, Vera. We'll be having class at seven."

"Oh, good. I was worried that with the

tragedy and all, you might have decided to cancel."

I distinctly remembered leaving a message on Vera's answering machine, but I knew firsthand how fickle electronic devices could be. "Nope. We're still on."

Vera smiled. "I'm glad. I'm sorry for what happened to Timothy, of course, but I've been looking forward to this class." She lifted and dropped her shoulders. "I've been searching for a creative outlet, if you will."

"Well, I hope you'll be pleased with the class and that it gives you the opportunity to tap into your artistic side."

"I do, too," Vera said with a girlish giggle. "I signed up for the cross-stitch tote bag project."

"Oh, that's great. Since the holidays are coming up in a couple of months, I thought we could make some as gifts. You know, either for ourselves or our friends and relatives, or to give to the women's shelter or girls' club."

"Or all of the above!"

I laughed at Vera's enthusiasm. "Then I'd better get to the shop early and make sure I have enough supplies."

Less than two hours later, I was surveying my eager group. Vera, the most eager, was sitting on the edge of her seat with an open notebook on her lap. Reggie Singh sat beside her, and Mrs. Trelawney sat beside Reggie. On the other navy sofa, the honey-haired girl who'd developed such a rapport with Angus sat beside her mother. Angus sat at the girl's feet with his head resting on her knee. I later learned the girl's name was Amber and her mother was Julie. I sat on the red chair with my materials spread out on the ottoman.

"For this project," I said, "we're going to cross-stitch a design on a canvas tote bag." I held up a couple of the bags. "As you can see, these come in a variety of colors, or you can choose the natural color. Either way, our first order of business is to use a fabric marker to create a cross-stitch grid where we'll be making our design."

Vera wrote furiously in her notebook, and Mrs. Trelawney asked for directions to the bathroom.

As Mrs. Trelawney ambled off, I said, "You can choose the color of your tote bag based on the pattern you like." I'd directed the comment to Amber, thinking the girl might want a tote in bright pink or fluorescent green. She merely looked a little blankly at me, but Vera wrote the comment down, making me feel it must've been important after all.

Mrs. Trelawney finally wandered back to rejoin the group. She settled onto the sofa and bestowed a smile on everyone — including Angus. In a *Peanuts*-inspired fantasy, I pictured Mrs. Trelawney asking, "Who's the kid with the dog-biscuit breath, sir? He needs a haircut, but he sure can embroider."

I shook off the image and directed everyone to choose a pattern. "If you haven't done cross-stitch before, let me know and I'll be happy to help you find a pattern that won't be too challenging your first time out."

Everyone got up and went to look at patterns. Everyone, that is, except Mrs. Trelawney.

"Would you like me to help you pick out a pattern, Mrs. Trelawney?"

"Oh, no, thank you, dear. I'll just watch and talk . . . and have punch and cookies."

I slowly bobbed my head and made a mental inventory of what I had in my desk that could conceivably constitute punch and cookies. Where had Mrs. Trelawney gotten the idea there would be refreshments served at this class? With a stiff smile, I excused myself and went to rifle through my desk. I found a box of oatmeal-raisin granola bars. It was a full box, and I could cut the bars into tiny squares. In my mini fridge, there was some mango juice. Since I had plates, napkins, and cups left over from the open house, I could improvise. By the time everyone — everyone but Mrs. Trelawney — had chosen a cross-stitch pattern, I had refreshments spread out on the counter.

As soon as Mrs. Trelawney had sampled the "cookies and punch," she informed me that "the cookies are a little tough, but the punch tastes just like mango juice. I like it."

I thanked her and returned to teaching the class. An hour full of happy chatter and flying fingers later, I'd helped four of my students make cross-stitch grids on their tote bags. And Mrs. Trelawney had drunk all the "punch." All in all, I suppose it was a successful class.

My first customer the next morning was Vera Langhorne.

"I couldn't wait to show you what I got done after I went home last night. John had a council meeting, so he didn't get home until late. That gave me plenty of time to cross-stitch." She spread her fuchsia tote bag out on the counter. "What do you think?"

Vera's design was a teapot, cup, and saucer. So far, she had the middle row and the two rows above it completed.

"That's coming together really nicely, Vera."

Vera beamed like a child who'd received a giant smiley face on her homework. "Can I stay here and work for a while? That way, if I hit any snags, you'll be here to help me."

"Of course," I said with a smile. "In fact, I'll join you." I took my tote bag, pattern, and thread and joined Vera in the sitting area. My pattern was a likeness of Angus' scruffy head. I'd made the pattern using a photograph of Angus that had been cropped and copied onto graph paper.

"Does it give you the willies to be here alone now?" Vera asked.

"Not really. Besides, I always have Angus here with me."

"That's true."

"The whole ordeal does boggle the mind, though. It was obvious Mr. Enright was drunk at the open house, although everyone who knew him said he never drank a drop. Then his wife shows up at my house, threatening to sue me." I shook my head. "It's been a stressful week."

"That's an understatement," Vera said. "But don't mind Lorraine Enright — she's just a bag of hot air. She'd been after Timothy for years to move his store to either somewhere in California or at least Portland, but Timothy wouldn't budge. I'd have thought she'd see his business closing as an opportunity to finally get what she'd been wanting."

"She didn't?"

"No. She up and left Timothy high and dry after twenty-five years of marriage."

"There had to be something else going on there."

"You never know with Lorraine. As a matter of fact, she might've left in order to force Timothy's hand on whatever it was she wanted this time."

"You mean she'd left him before?" I asked.

Vera nodded. "That woman probably has a PhD in manipulation."

She was quiet for a moment, and I could tell she was counting her stitches. Then Vera looked up and grinned. "Like I said, don't let Lorraine get to you."

"I'll try. By the way, do you know what *four square fifth w* could mean?"

"Possibly." She frowned. "Four Square is — or, rather, was — a development company. The owners went to jail last year."

"For what?"

"Fraud. They were in cahoots with a real estate appraiser who was giving them inflated property appraisals."

I sat back in my chair. "Do you think Timothy Enright could've known something about that?"

"I'm sure he did. It was the talk of Tallulah Falls for months. It upset John terribly. He's a banker, you know."

"No, that's not what I meant. Do you think Mr. Enright might've known something that could have implicated someone else?"

Vera raised her brows. "I don't know. I suppose he could have."

Vera and I worked in companionable silence until the bell above the shop door signaled the arrival of another customer. I turned and was somewhat surprised to see Ted Nash walk in.

"Hello, Detective. How may I help you?"

"Is there somewhere we can speak privately?"

Vera began stuffing her work into a sewing bag. "That's okay, Ted. I need to get home and start dinner. You can have my spot here on the sofa."

"I'm sorry to inconvenience you, Mrs. Langhorne."

"No trouble at all. Marcy, see you later." Vera gave Angus a pat on the head before she left.

Detective Nash nodded toward the dog.

"Can you do something with him? He makes me uncomfortable."

I bit back a smart-alecky retort and put Angus in the bathroom. When I returned, the detective had indeed taken Vera's place on the sofa. I remained standing. "I hope this won't take long. Angus hates being shut in the bathroom."

"It shouldn't take but a few minutes. I would like you to sit down, though."

I took a seat on the edge of the sofa across from Detective Nash. Somehow it made me feel better to have the coffee table between us.

"I understand from Mrs. Trelawney that her husband intended to stop by here yesterday," the detective said. "Did you see him?"

"Actually, no. I'd taken Angus for a walk and left Sadie MacKenzie in charge. She mentioned that he dropped in but didn't stay long."

Detective Nash jotted down some information in his notebook. "I'll speak with her about his visit. Mrs. Trelawney indicated you'd called Mr. Trelawney the day before yesterday. Is that correct?"

"Yes."

"Would you care to disclose the nature of your call?"

"I don't see why not. I called Mr. Trelawney to see if he knew why Mr. Enright closed his business. Mrs. Enright indicated that Mr. Trelawney was seeking more artistic shops in the plaza."

"And what was Mr. Trelawney's response?"

I shrugged. "He said that was ridiculous."

"Is that all?"

"No. I mentioned what Mr. Enright had scratched onto the wall. It seemed to upset him, and that's when he said he'd be in to take a look at it. It just so happened he came while Sadie was here."

"And did Mrs. MacKenzie say anything about Mr. Trelawney's visit?"

"Only that he was freaked-out about the writing on the wall and wanted it painted over as soon as possible."

"Okay. Thank you for your time, Ms. Singer. I'll step next door and speak with Mrs. MacKenzie now. If you think of anything else, you have my card. Right?"

"Right. Um . . . why all the questions about Mr. Trelawney?"

Detective Nash hesitated, then sighed. "You'll hear about it soon enough, anyway. Mr. Trelawney is dead. He was found shot to death in his car about an hour ago."

I gasped. "Are you serious?"

"No, Ms. Singer, I enjoy joking about such things. Of course I'm serious. Where were you earlier this morning?"

"I've been here since ten a.m. Vera has been here the past hour or so."

He nodded. "You have no plans to leave town, do you?"

"Of course not!"

"Good. See that you don't."

CHAPTER FOUR

I hurried to the bathroom as soon as Detective Nash left. My intention was to let Angus out. But when I opened the door, I sank to my knees on the floor and pulled the dog to me. I was trembling, and he began licking my neck and chin.

I heard the bell above the door jingle, but I wanted to regain my composure before facing any customers.

"Marcy?"

That voice was unmistakable. It was Todd's.

"Just a sec." I stood and smoothed my khakis. When I went back out front, I found Todd casually leaning against the counter in faded jeans and a red V-neck sweater.

I grinned. "Was Jill keeping you company?"

He tilted his head. "She's not much of a conversationalist."

"She's just a little shy until you get to

know her."

"Hey, buddy." Todd patted Angus' head. "Saw Ted Nash making the rounds. Has he got anything new?"

I took a deep breath. "I'll say he does. Let's have a seat." I stepped around the counter, and Todd joined me in the sitting area. We both took a seat on the navy sofa that faced the windows.

"Bill Trelawney was found shot to death in his car earlier today," I said.

"What? You've got to be kidding." Todd paled visibly.

"I wish I were."

"So, Nash is going door-to-door questioning each of Bill's tenants?"

"I don't know." But the thought occurred to me that he might be doing just that. "Maybe." I rested my head against the back of the sofa. "If so, he started with me because Mr. Trelawney came by here yesterday morning." I closed my eyes. "I called to see if Mr. Trelawney might know anything about why Lorraine Enright thinks I put her husband . . . ex-husband . . ." I opened my eyes and looked at Todd. "Estranged husband?"

"Tim."

"Right. Anyway, I called him to ask why Mrs. Enright thinks I put Tim out of busi-

77

ness. After I told him what Tim had scratched onto the storeroom wall, he became a little upset and said he'd come by to look at it."

"What did Tim scratch onto the wall?"

"*Four square fifth w.* Mean anything to you?"

Todd shook his head. "No. But it must've meant something to Bill Trelawney."

"Vera Langhorne told me Four Square was the name of a development company at one time and that some of its members went to jail. Maybe Mr. Trelawney made a connection between Four Square Development and Mr. Enright's scribbles."

"I suppose anything's possible. Did Bill Trelawney say anything about it before he left?"

"Not to me. I'd taken Angus for a quick walk, and Sadie was minding the shop."

"Which explains why Nash hurried next door."

"Exactly. Now two people connected with my shop are dead. I'm afraid to ask what's next."

From our vantage point, we could see Detective Nash getting into his car. He hadn't had time to get out of sight before Sadie burst into the shop.

"Can you believe it?" she asked breathlessly. "Who'd want to kill poor old Mr. Trelawney?"

"Maybe the same person who killed Timothy Enright," I said.

Sadie flopped onto the sofa across from Todd and me. "From the way Ted talked, Chief Myers isn't ruling out either of us as suspects."

"He thinks one of us killed Mr. Trelawney?" I asked.

"And Tim Enright." She sighed. "This can't be happening."

I was scared. One man — the man who for thirty years had leased the very same shop I now leased — had died in my storeroom from what police believed was poisoning. Another man — my landlord — had died hours after visiting my storeroom. Now, I could make myself believe there was something toxic in the storeroom — something even the hazmat crew had failed to contain and that had poisoned Timothy Enright and maybe even Bill Trelawney. Although the fact that Bill Trelawney had been shot completely annihilated that theory. A contagious pocket of really bad luck was starting to seem on the money, though.

I closed up the store at five and then headed home. I dropped Angus off and he was playing in the backyard, but I found myself merely pacing around the living room. I had to at least try to find some answers. I called the library and learned they were open until six thirty p.m. Maybe I could find some answers there.

The library was a large brick Victorian structure just about a mile outside town. When I walked in, I noticed the cozy seating area in a room to my right. Two weathered leather sofas and some oversize chairs scattered throughout the room made the perfect reading nook. To my left was a larger room with a circulation desk and floor-to-ceiling bookshelves.

Reggie Singh was shelving books in this room when I arrived. She wore another tunic ensemble today. This one was turquoise and had multicolored beadwork on the collar and down the sides of the pants. I wondered if she'd done the beadwork herself, but I had more pressing questions to ask.

"Hi there, Marcy." She smiled. "Are you looking for anything in particular today?"

"As a matter of fact, I am." I glanced at the man reading a newspaper at a table to my right. A few other people were browsing the shelves. "Is there somewhere we can talk privately?"

"Sure. Follow me." She took the cart back to the circulation desk and told a young woman sitting there that we would be in her office.

Reggie led me down a narrow hallway and into an office. The office was eclectically decorated with Indian art mixed with framed photographs of the coast. Somehow it seemed to work.

Reggie closed the door and sat down behind her mahogany desk. "What's on your mind?"

I sank into the armless Victorian silk-covered chair to the side of the desk. "I'm scared."

Reggie nodded thoughtfully. "Manu told me about Bill Trelawney."

"Two people with connections to my shop, dead within a matter of days? Who's to say I won't be next?"

"Let's not rush to conclusions. Two men with connections to *Timothy Enright's* shop are dead, and the police aren't even sure the deaths are related."

"What do you think?" I asked. "I mean, you've lived in this town for years; you knew Timothy Enright well. What would you do if you were me?"

She spread her hands. "If I were you, I'd keep that enormous dog by my side at all

81

times." She pushed her glasses up. "As for what I think . . . I think we need to find out what's going on."

"So you do think the deaths are related."

Reggie shrugged. "Pray for the best. Prepare for the worst. Manu said Bill Trelawney came to see you yesterday morning."

"He did. He wanted to see what Mr. Enright had scratched onto the wall with a tapestry needle."

"Four something, right?" Reggie took a legal pad from her middle desk drawer.

"Four square fifth w."

With a lavender pen, Reggie wrote this information on the rose-colored pad. I had to give her points for style.

"Vera Langhorne told me Four Square was the name of a development company," I continued. "She said some of the people involved went to jail for fraud."

"I remember that. Do you think Timothy Enright was trying to tell you something about Four Square Development?"

It was my turn to shrug. "I guess anything's possible. He did keep trying to talk to me at the party that night. He said there was something I needed to know."

"But you never found out what?"

"I'm afraid not." I clamped my lips together. "I . . . I avoided him. I really did think he was drunk, and —"

"It's okay," Reggie interrupted. "Your actions were perfectly understandable." She tapped her pad with the barrel of her pen. "It just makes our job a little harder. Let's start with Four Square and see where that takes us." Reggie took me to the computer room, did a search, and set me up with all the local newspaper articles for the months surrounding the indictments and trial of Four Square Development, since the local newspaper's Web site required a subscription fee and password to access content more than three months old. She had to get back to work, but said she'd check on me in a bit. She also left me the rose-colored paper and the pen with the lavender ink. Sweet.

The blue fabric chair I sat in was fairly comfy, but I had a feeling my butt was going to get awfully tired before my work here was done. I began scanning through the screens.

Twenty minutes into my search, I found a newspaper article with a Four Square mention. Since the newspapers were in reverse chronological order, I got the one with the sentencing information first. None of the names — Douglas Alexander, Norman Patrick, Paul Kerr, and Matthew Grant —

meant anything to me . . . except that three of the four had two first names rather than a first and last name. Of course, Kerr could be a German first name, so I suppose they all could have two first names.

Anyway, the sentences were relatively light. Each man had been given thirty-six months of prison time and had been ordered to pay one-fourth of the $925,000 restitution.

I scrolled through the newspaper articles until I found Four Square on the front page. It was the day after the trial. According to this report, evidence presented at trial showed the four partners were guilty of mortgage fraud.

Prosecutors allege the men, operating under the name Four Square Development, sold real estate using inflated appraisals. The properties were then sold to "straw buyers," who, it is believed, received kickbacks from the excess loan proceeds.

Reggie peeped around the door. "How are you coming along?"

"Do any of these names mean anything to you?" I turned the pink pad toward her.

"A couple of them do. Kerr and Patrick

were from here in town. The other two were from Seattle."

"Did Kerr or Patrick have any dealings with Timothy Enright?"

"I don't know. Patrick is — was — an attorney. He handled Four Square's closings." Reggie cocked her head. "I suppose he could have done Tim's will. He did mine and Manu's. He was a good attorney. Too bad he got involved with Four Square."

"Who took over his business?"

"His partner, Riley Kendall."

I turned the pad back around and wrote down the new information.

"Don't expect Riley to confide much," Reggie said. "She's Norm Patrick's daughter."

I left the library at just past six p.m. and decided to take a chance that Riley Kendall might still be in her office.

The office door still bore the words PATRICK AND KENDALL, ATTORNEYS AT LAW. Either Riley hadn't gotten around to changing it during the past several months, or her dad was hoping to get his law license reinstated after he'd served his time. I opened the door, and a chime sounded. It wasn't a friendly little jingle like the bells over my shop door. This was more like a doorbell or a muted gong.

"Good afternoon. May I help you?" The cultured voice came from my left and belonged to a woman with gray-streaked hair pulled into a severe bun. For some reason, her appearance made me feel like a child . . . a child who should be seen and not heard. Accordingly, I spoke as softly as I could without actually whispering.

"May I please see Riley Kendall?"

"Ms. Kendall is with a client at the moment. Would you care to leave a message?"

"I'd like to wait, if you don't think she'll be very much longer."

"You may have a seat in the reception area."

I thought I was already in the reception area, but I mumbled a "thank you" and carefully stepped across the Oriental rug to the floral brocade sofa. Riley may not have changed the firm's name, but I had to wonder if she'd redecorated the offices in her father's absence. This room, at least, had a strong feminine presence. Wingback chairs brought out the rose color in the sofa, and a designer floral arrangement in the center of the highly polished cherry table beautifully highlighted the rest of the sofa's muted tones. The room made me think of my aunt June. She was an interior designer

— the love of fabrics runs in our family. Aunt June used to always say, "Buy your couch, and I'll build your room around it."

I turned my head at the sound of voices. One of them seemed familiar. The two women had their backs to me, but I could see that one was a brunette in a pale blue suit and the other had red hair like . . .

She suddenly faced me. Yep. Lorraine Enright.

Her eyes narrowed. "What are you doing here? Are you following me?"

"No, Mrs. Enright. I'm here to see Ms. Kendall."

Lorraine whirled back to Riley. "Don't you dare tell her a thing we talked about — do you hear me? Not a thing!"

"That goes without saying, Lorraine," the woman I assumed must be Riley said calmly. "Attorney-client privilege, remember?"

"I remember. Just see that you do." With that, she stormed out of the office.

I rose from the sofa, and Riley met me halfway. She held out her hand. "Riley Kendall. What can I do for you?"

I shook her hand. "Hi. I'm Marcy Singer." Glancing at the receptionist, I asked if we could speak privately. The receptionist glared at me.

"Sure. Mom, hold my calls for a few

minutes, please."

Inwardly, I groaned. Somehow, I'd managed to infuriate one of this woman's clients and insult her mother within a mere five minutes of meeting her. Even for me, that had to be some sort of record.

"Don't forget," said Riley's mom, "we need to pay Margaret Trelawney a visit later this evening."

Before she'd left the shop, Sadie had suggested that she and I visit Mrs. Trelawney tonight, as well. I glanced at my watch and realized I needed to hurry if I was going to be on time to meet Sadie.

"It won't take long," I said as Riley ushered me into her office.

The office was similar to the reception area. The same color scheme was used, and I could see touches provided by the same floral designer. A flower arrangement sat on a tall cherry table beneath the window, and one of the blooms had been carried over to a bud vase at the corner of Riley's desk. There were framed photographs on the bookshelves and walls. Some featured a handsome man in his early thirties, but many depicted a balding middle-aged man.

I nodded toward one of the more prominent photos. "Your dad?"

Riley nodded, and a wistful expression flitted across her face. She immediately got to business. "How can I help you, Marcy?"

"You might know that I just opened the embroidery shop on Emerson Street. The one where Timothy Enright had his hardware store, and where he, well, died."

She nodded.

"On the night Timothy Enright died, he scratched the words *four square fifth* onto my wall with a tapestry needle."

Riley frowned, but said nothing.

"I'm wondering if by *four square,* he meant Four Square Development."

Riley sat back in her chair and folded her hands. "It's my understanding that Mr. Enright appeared disoriented and confused that evening."

"He was slurring his words and staggering, but we now believe that was because he'd been poisoned."

"*We* being you and your team of medical experts?"

I leaned forward. "Look, two people within a week visited my storeroom and later died. I think their deaths are connected."

"I don't —"

"As a legal expert whose father was a part of Four Square Development, I thought you, of all people, might be interested in helping me sort this out."

"This has nothing to do with my father."

"Are you sure?" I stood and moved toward the door. "Because whoever killed Timothy Enright and Bill Trelawney might not be finished. If you decide to lend a hand, let me know."

I returned to the Jeep on shaky legs. I hadn't expected too much help from Riley Kendall given the circumstances, but knowing she was an associate of Lorraine Enright made her antagonism even worse. Riley was in the perfect position to know — or to find out — if Timothy Enright had anything to do with Four Square Development.

I arrived home with more time to spare than I'd expected. I was tired, but I wanted to relax for a few minutes before heading out again.

I left Angus outside in the fenced-in yard and went upstairs to the bedroom. I took out the replica of the MacKenzies' Mochas logo I was stitching, kicked off my shoes, and leaned back against the pillows. The light streaming through the bedroom was fantastic, so I didn't need to turn on my nightstand lamp just yet. I was planning to give the logo to Sadie and Blake as a

Christmas present, so I couldn't work on it at the shop.

The MacKenzies' Mochas logo is a huge, tan coffee cup with a pale melon stripe. Smoke from the hot coffee is swirling up from the cup. MACKENZIES' is written over top of it and MOCHAS below it in ivory. The background is a dark wood grain, reminiscent of an old tavern sign.

I was copying the logo from a photograph I took of the MacKenzies' sign. I'd been working on the design for a month now. So far, I had the top third of the sign completed, but it was slow going. I had needles in three different colors threaded to help me keep up with the frequent color changes. It was nice to see it starting to come together, though.

Three full lines into the design, I glanced at the clock. I'd been working for half an hour. I folded the fabric around the embroidery hoop and placed it back into the nightstand drawer.

I quickly showered and changed. After feeding Angus and taking him for another quick jaunt outside, I went to MacKenzies' Mochas to meet Sadie. Blake had fixed up a basket of muffins and scones for us to take to Mrs. Trelawney.

"I dread this," Sadie confided as she got

into the Jeep. "I might've been the last person to see Mr. Trelawney alive."

"I don't think so."

"Oh . . . I know. Geesh."

"I didn't mean just the murderer." I started the engine. "There were probably lots of people Mr. Trelawney visited before . . . Before."

"That's true. His death might not even be connected to you or to Timothy Enright. I mean, it could've been a robbery gone wrong. That's what Chief Myers believes."

"A robbery gone wrong in the middle of the day?"

"It's possible. I overheard some people talking at the shop, and apparently Mr. Trelawney was pretty far out of town, near some deserted old buildings."

"Then that makes it even less likely it was a robbery gone wrong, Sadie. I mean, what possible reason would Mr. Trelawney have for going to some deserted old buildings?"

"He *was* a landlord. Maybe he was thinking about buying them and renovating them." She looked over at me. "But I'm guessing you have another theory."

I checked my rearview mirror and then backed out of the parking spot. "I do have another theory. I think he was meeting someone who was involved with Four

Square Development. You said yourself he was acting completely out of character, and I could tell when I spoke with him that he was really upset about the four square message being scratched onto the wall."

"I mean, Marcy, the guy was a landlord. Maybe he didn't like that someone defaced his property."

"Really?" I asked. "Is that really what you think?"

She didn't answer.

"Neither do I," I said.

CHAPTER FIVE

The Trelawney house was already crowded by the time Sadie and I arrived. When we got inside, I looked around for both Mrs. Trelawney and Riley Kendall. I didn't see either one. I was rather relieved not to see Riley and rather concerned not to see Mrs. Trelawney.

A woman who appeared to be in her mid to late sixties, with what the women of *Steel Magnolias* would've called a football-helmet hairdo, greeted us and thanked us for coming.

"Where's Mrs. Trelawney?" I asked.

The woman thinned her already thin lips. "She's sitting in the den. She was blubbering and babbling so much, I sent her in there."

"And who are you?" Sadie asked with her customary tact.

"I'm Sylvia Shaw, Bill's sister. I'm here to see to his affairs. Maggie certainly isn't capable of doing so."

"Where's the den?" I asked.

"Down the hall, second door on your right."

"Thank you."

"What nerve," Sadie whispered as we started down the hall.

"Poor Mrs. Trelawney. First her husband dies, and then she has to deal with this shrew." I knocked quietly on the den door.

"Come in," came the muffled answer from inside the room.

I opened the door, and Sadie and I stepped into the room. There were no lights on, so we had to adjust our eyes to the dim light filtering in from the hallway. The den had two walls covered with bookshelves. The books were all hardcovers, and most of them appeared to be old, as far as I could tell. A large desk sat in the middle of the room, and there were two brown leather couches facing each other from either side of the desk. Mrs. Trelawney lay on the couch that was facing away from the door.

I closed the door halfway, hoping we wouldn't be disturbed but needing the glimmer of light. "Mrs. Trelawney, it's Marcy Singer and Sadie MacKenzie. Are you all right?"

"No, my dears. How could I be all right?"

Sadie and I shared a glance and then approached Mrs. Trelawney.

"We're so sorry," I said.

"Blake and I made some of your favorite muffins and scones today," Sadie said. "Before we go, I'll put this basket in the kitchen."

"Thank you."

"Is there anything we can do for you, Mrs. Trelawney?" I asked. "Anything you need us to get for you?"

"Anyone we can call for you?" Sadie added.

Mrs. Trelawney smiled wanly. "Somebody besides Sylvia, you mean?"

"Yeah," Sadie said. "She's a real piece of work."

"She has a brusque way about her, but she means well."

Sadie frowned. "But she sent you —"

"To my room — or, rather, Bill's room — like a misbehaving little child?" Mrs. Trelawney asked. "She thought it was best. I was terribly distressed."

"No one would expect you to be otherwise," I said.

Mrs. Trelawney raised a white lace handkerchief to her cheek. "Why would anyone want to hurt Bill? He's a good man."

"We know." I patted her hand. "I can't

help but wonder if his death and Timothy Enright's death are somehow connected."

She started when I said that, and looked straight at me, her eyes brighter. It was as if she'd suddenly come out of a dream. "Do you think so? I told Chief Myers that, but he didn't seem to agree. It's so terrible, so awful to think . . . but I've been wondering, too. I don't want to . . ."

Suddenly, the den door was flung open and the light flipped on. Mrs. Trelawney, Sadie, and I blinked and squinted against the glare.

"Maggie," Sylvia said, "Detective Nash is here to see you, so please straighten up and answer his questions."

Detective Nash shot Sylvia a look of disbelief before she turned as stiffly as a toy soldier and exited the den.

"Good evening," Detective Nash said to Mrs. Trelawney. "I'm sorry to disturb you at this terrible time, Mrs. Trelawney, but I need to ask you a few questions." He looked at Sadie and me. "Would you please excuse us, ladies?"

"Of course," Sadie said. "I need to put this basket in the kitchen."

"And I'd like to see if Mrs. Danvers has a reflection in the mirror over the mantel in the living room," I said.

I was surprised to see Detective Nash's lips twitch at that. Was it possible he knew who Mrs. Danvers was? He might have a tiny bit of a sense of humor after all.

Sadie and I took the muffin and scone basket through the small groups of people gathered throughout the living room into the adjoining dining room. A man and woman stood near the head of a large walnut dining table, discussing the stock market as if they were at a cocktail party. We excused ourselves and walked by them into the kitchen. There were several food baskets sitting on the island. Three were fruit baskets, two contained cookies, and one held meats and cheeses. Sadie placed her basket among the others.

"Maggie will never be able to eat all that fruit before it spoils," Sylvia said.

She'd been standing quietly in the corner, and I hadn't noticed her. I don't think Sadie had, either.

"Would one of you girls please remove the cards from two of those fruit baskets and then take the fruit to the food bank tomorrow?" Sylvia asked.

Sadie and I exchanged glances. It seemed terribly inappropriate to visit a grieving widow and make off with her fruit baskets . . . even if we were giving the baskets to the poor. I mean, not even Robin Hood would be that audacious. Would he?

"The cards will convey the well-wishers' sentiments," Sylvia continued, "and the fruit will go to a good cause rather than sit here and rot."

"You've got a point," Sadie said.

"Of course, I do. I'm not an ogre. I'm trying to take care of things." Sylvia's eyes filled with tears. "Billy was my big brother, and he always took care of me. Now I have to —" Her voice broke, and she began to sob.

"We're truly sorry for your loss," I said.

"Yes, we are." Sadie began taking the cards off two of the fruit baskets. "We have no idea what you and Mrs. Trelawney must be going through."

"If there's anything you need . . . anything we can do," I began lamely, "please let us know." Why is it that even the most heartfelt sentiments expressed at times like this seem so trite?

Sylvia sniffled. "Just drop off the fruit baskets, please."

"We will." I looked pointedly toward the dining room. "Do you mind if we go out this back door, in case the people who brought these baskets are still here?"

"Not at all." Sylvia took a tissue from the

pocket of her tailored black jacket and wiped away the mascara smudged under her eyes. "Thank you."

With Sadie and I each carrying a fruit basket, we furtively slipped out the kitchen door. As we started around the side of the house, we heard voices. I put my free hand on Sadie's arm to cue her to stop.

"She told me Tim wrote something about Four Square on her wall."

That was Riley Kendall.

"What was he doing there, Lorraine?" Riley continued. "Why would he want to tell Marcy Singer anything? Did he even know her?"

"Not that I know of," said Lorraine Enright. "I don't think he was cheating on me with her, if that's what you mean."

"That's not what I mean at all," Riley said. "I'm really not trying to pry into your love life. What I want — what I need — to know is what and how Tim knew about Four Square."

"I'll look through his papers again," Lorraine said. "That's all I can do."

I jerked my head toward the other side of the house. Sadie nodded, and we went in the opposite direction from Riley and Lorraine.

"Wonder what that was about," Sadie said

as soon as we got into the Jeep.

I told her about my visit to Riley's office earlier that afternoon.

"What now?" Sadie asked.

"I don't know. Maybe Reggie can help me figure out why Tim Enright wanted to talk with me about Four Square."

"Or maybe Norman Patrick can."

I shot her a quick look. "Riley's dad?"

"Uh-huh. The prison isn't that far from here. We could pay him a visit on Sunday."

"We as in *you and I?"*

"We could take Blake and Todd along and make a day of it."

"Oh, sure, Sadie, that would be cool. Road trip to the penitentiary. That sounds like such a fun time, I'm surprised no one has made a movie about it. I'll see if Mom can talk it up around some of her friends."

Sadie was silent. "Wait," I said. "You're serious, aren't you?"

"Of course I'm serious."

"But what makes you think Norman Patrick would even talk with us?"

"Because old Norm was rumored to be quite the womanizer. And I've heard it said the gentleman prefers blondes." She softly tugged a strand of my hair.

I rolled my eyes. But then I thought about it. I figured it couldn't hurt, and I certainly didn't have any other leads in the murder for which I apparently figured prominently on the suspect list. Oh, great. I turned to Sadie. "Then we're off to the big house. Are you sure Blake and Todd will come along?"

She uttered a low, throaty chuckle. "When I tell Blake we're headed to a minimum-security prison where men have been locked away from women for months on end, he'll be in the car before I can finish my sentence."

"And Todd?"

"Oh, he'd come spend the day with you if we were going to a landfill."

I giggled, secretly hoping she was right. "How about Paul Kerr? Is he at the same prison as Mr. Patrick?"

"I'm afraid not. I believe he's a little farther upstate."

When I got home, I locked the front door behind me, let Angus in, and both locked and dead-bolted the back door. Maybe I was being overly cautious. But better overly cautious than dead.

There were two messages on my answering machine. One was from Mom, and the other was from Detective Nash. I decided to call Mom. If anything else bad had happened, I didn't want to know it yet.

"Hello, Beverly Singer," Mom answered, her voice trilling *Singer* as if perhaps that was her profession.

She always answers the phone professionally because "you never know who might be calling." I've tried to tell her that's what caller ID is for, but she argues that it would ruin the surprise.

"Hi, Mom."

"Darling, how are you? Has that business about the fellow in your storeroom been cleared up yet?"

"They're working on it."

"Good. And the classes . . . Are they being well received?"

"Yup. I'm delighted by the number of people who signed up and have actually been coming. How are things with you?"

"Fairly well. There's a nasty little diva on the set whose costumes never measure up to her inflated expectations — she doesn't even have a starring role, for goodness' sake — but everyone else is a love. The men especially."

"Naturally. You could charm them into wearing paper sacks."

"That's not true. They simply respect me because they realize I'm excellent at my job."

At fifty-eight, Mom is still a looker. She

has silvery blond hair, dancing blue eyes, and a ready smile. She's kept her figure, too. Granted, it's more of a Jane Russell–eighteen-hour-bra figure than a Kate Moss figure, but I think that appeals to a lot of men. At least, it does in Mom's case.

"I suppose your expertise could be part of it," I said.

"Tell me about Tallulah Falls. Is it pretty there?"

"It's gorgeous, Mom. You'll have to come and see for yourself. There are these huge rocks out in the ocean that somehow make me think of *Wuthering Heights.*"

Mom laughed. "Ah, they bring to mind the crags out upon the moors, eh, Catherine?"

"Aye, and I suppose they do, Heathcliff. I suppose they do." I dropped the accent. "Wait a minute. *Wuthering Heights* took place in Yorkshire, England, not Ireland."

"Weel, faith, and begorra," she said, rolling those *R*s in *begorra* for all she was worth. "Why do ye want to be goin' and spoilin' our fun now, lassie?"

"Truth be tellin' ye, I'm not certain, Mother." I could roll *R*s with the best of them. "Only I know 'tis later here than there, and I must be gettin' up frightfully early tomorrow morn."

"I'll take my leave from ye then, me love. Hugs and kisses to me darlin' Angus now, ye hear?"

"Will do." I spoke normally. "I love you, Mom."

"I love you, too, sweetheart. Call me if you need anything, okay?"

"Um . . ."

"Um, what?" she asked. "That was a loaded *um* if I ever heard one."

"It's nothing. Really. I just . . . I love you, Mom."

"And everything is okay?"

"Yeah . . . sure. I just wanted to make sure you know."

"Of course I know. And you know I love you, too. When you're ready to talk about that *um,* give me a call back, okay?"

"All right."

When we hung up, I was feelin' a wee bit homesick for the Old Country . . . which for me was Mom's house in San Francisco. I didn't want to worry Mom any more than I already had, especially since she was on the other side of the country. But I felt guilty about keeping her in the dark about Mr. Trelawney. What if something *did* happen to me?

As much as I dreaded doing so, I called Detective Nash back. I was surprised to find that the number he'd left on my machine was his personal number rather than the police station's.

"Hi, Detective Nash," I said when he answered. "This is Marcy Singer returning your call."

"Hi, Marcy. I'm sorry I interrupted your visit with Margaret Trelawney this evening. It was police business. Couldn't be helped."

"That's fine. She's terribly distraught, as anyone would be."

"Of course. May I stop by the shop tomorrow?"

"Sure. Is there a particular reason?" I asked.

"I'd just like to look around a bit more."

I took a breath before taking the plunge. "Do you think the Enright and Trelawney murders are connected?"

"At this point, I'm not sure. I would like for you to remain hypervigilant until we know more about both these cases."

"Am I still a suspect in these murders?"

"I can't rule anyone out yet," he said, "but I personally think you're innocent. The chief will take some more convincing, though." He sighed. "You have no motive. I'm thinking whoever is responsible for these murders has lived here in Tallulah Falls for a very long time and has a history with these men."

"Do you think I'm in danger, Detective?"

"I don't know. But you do need to take extra precautionary measures for the time being. I'll have on-duty officers patrol your house and store periodically to provide further security."

"Thanks." I wondered if he knew how insecure all his talk about security was making me feel.

"Just doing our jobs. Call us anytime."

I thanked him again and hung up. It was weird that he'd asked if he could stop by the shop tomorrow. Every other time he'd wanted to come by the shop, he'd barged right on in. Something was up.

I climbed into bed, and Angus curled up at my feet. He does that sometimes. It's positively catlike, except that Angus is more puma-size.

The wind was blowing hard that night. It occasionally rattled the windows. A light flashed past one window and momentarily illuminated the bedroom. I tried to tell myself it was only a passing car and not a psycho with a gun.

I snuggled down into the bed and pulled the covers up around my ears. "I'm glad you're here, Angus. Otherwise, I might feel a little bit scared."

■ ■ ■ ■

It was going to be hard for me to get used to working every Saturday. At the accounting firm, I had to work Saturdays only during tax season, which is from January 2 through April 15. Some of the accountants absolutely loved tax season; they called it money season. But I absolutely hated it. What a drag. Work became our entire life during those three and a half months.

Anyway, this was my first Saturday as a small-business owner–slash–retail merchant, and I was looking forward to getting to work. Angus and I had a leisurely breakfast followed by a not-so-leisurely walk — he saw a ginger cat and wanted to chase it. Where's Cesar Millan when you need him?

I did leave early, as there was a stop I wanted to make before going to work. I opened my purse and removed the piece of notepad paper I'd taken from the library. I then took out my GPS and entered the second address I'd written on Reggie's legal pad.

1414 Cedar Avenue. Janelle Kerr.

When I got there, it appeared that Mrs. Kerr was leaving home for work. She was a slight woman dressed in a business suit, and she had dark blond hair and ever-watchful brown eyes.

"Mrs. Kerr," I called as I got out of the Jeep, leaving Angus inside with the windows cracked. "Do you have a moment?"

"For what?" she asked.

By this time, I'd reached the walk and could lower my voice. "I'd like to talk with you about your husband and Four Square Development."

She shook her head. "I told you reporters the last time you were here that I don't have anything to say to you."

"I'm not a reporter," I said. "My name is Marcy Singer. I'm here because Timothy Enright died in my storeroom."

Still unwilling to allow me into her home, Mrs. Kerr invited me to sit with her on the patio. She had a white, wrought-iron bistro set sitting near a gas grill.

"Please sit down," she said.

I sat on one of the pretty but uncomfortable chairs, and she sat on the other.

"You'll excuse me for not inviting you inside," she said. "I don't trust people very much these days."

"I can't say that I blame you. Did you know Timothy Enright?"

"Only in passing. I didn't patronize the hardware shop that often." She took a cigarette and lighter from her purse. "Why would you think his death would have anything to do with my husband or Four Square Development? Paul has been incarcerated for nearly a year; and as far as I know, Four Square Development is defunct."

"I don't know much about Four Square Development or Mr. Enright, but I do believe his death might have been because of something he was involved in or knew concerning Four Square."

She lit the cigarette and blew a puff of smoke over her shoulder. "How did you arrive at that conclusion?"

"Mr. Enright scratched *four square fifth w* on my storeroom wall with a tapestry needle before he died. After Bill Trelawney saw the wall, he was upset over it. Later that day he, too, was found dead."

"Yes, I'm aware of Mr. Trelawney's death. I was sorry to hear about that."

"Did your husband know Bill Trelawney?"

She nodded, taking a long draw from her cigarette. "Paul was Mr. Trelawney's accountant. He prepared Mr. Trelawney's tax returns and that sort of thing."

"But your husband never mentioned Timothy Enright in connection with Four Square Development?"

"No, but then, we didn't talk about Four Square Development. He kept most of his business dealings to himself." She flipped her hand. "You know the old adage: Leave work at work."

"But Four Square wasn't a typical venture," I said.

"Even so, Paul kept his involvement to himself."

"What about the other men?" I asked. "Do you think any of them might know or be willing to discuss whether Timothy Enright or Bill Trelawney had any connection with Four Square Development?"

"I doubt it." She took one last puff off her cigarette before crushing it out under her boot. "Look. These men — Paul included — want to serve their time and put Four Square Development as far away from themselves as they can. Four Square Development has ruined them. They'll never have the careers they had before . . . never hold the community's trust and respect. This mistake will hang over their heads forever." She picked up the cigarette butt and tossed it into the bushes. "Frankly, I doubt any of them care much about either Timothy Enright or Bill Trelawney, or whether either of them — or both of them, for that matter — was involved with Four Square Development. It's irrelevant to them."

"Maybe so," I said. "But it's not irrelevant to me. I need to know why two men are dead and if their deaths are in any way connected with my shop." She inclined her head away from me. Clearly, she wasn't willing to say any more. I stood. "Thank you for your time, Mrs. Kerr."

As I was walking to the Jeep, she called to me. "I'll talk with Paul and see if he knows anything."

I turned. "Thank you." I hurried back to give her my business card. "Thank you so much."

When Angus and I got to the store, a delivery man had just arrived with a huge box. What timing! I unlocked the door while holding an excited, box-sniffing Angus at bay.

"He loves packages," I explained to the bemused delivery man. "Sometimes my mom sends us care packages." I opened the door. "Would you mind bringing that inside please?"

"Not at all."

He took my "inside" direction quite literally, dropping the package inches within the door. I guess we'd taken up enough of his time. I gave him a tip, and he hurried on his way.

I unleashed Angus, and he sniffed the box again before wandering off into the store. Remembering the lift-with-your-legs drill, I bent and tried to pick up the box. Yikes, that sucker was heavy. I didn't recall ordering any anvils. I looked at the label. JACKSON EMBROIDERY SUPPLY COMPANY. That would be my Halloween stuff. This box could not possibly be as heavy as it wanted me to believe it was. I wiped my palms down the sides of my jeans and prepared for Attempt Number Two. I bent and wrapped my arms around the box.

The door jingled, and Ted Nash walked in. He was almost smiling. And if that wasn't strange enough, he was wearing jeans, a long-sleeved T-shirt, and sneakers. Yes, actual running shoes — or maybe cross-trainers — but definitely not police or detective shoes.

"Wow," I said. "You look human . . . I mean, normal." Yeah, not my best conversational moment. But he caught me off guard. I was still thinking about how to move the box.

He did seem to take my comment in stride, though. "Wow," he said. "You look weak . . . I mean, pathetic. I'd be glad to carry that to the storeroom for you."

Normally, my pride would've caused me

to say something stupid like, "That's okay. I can handle it." Fortunately, I didn't have much pride left after the "you look normal" comment. So I merely stepped aside and thanked the man for his help.

When Angus saw us heading toward the storeroom, he bounded right over.

I looked up at Detective Nash. "Ever since Timothy Enright's accident, Angus loves to snoop around the storeroom." I gave an involuntary shiver. "It kinda creeps me out."

"Why did you name him Angus?" Detective Nash asked. "Are you a fan of AC/DC?"

"A little, but it's mainly because of his Irish heritage."

I opened the storeroom door, and Detective Nash set the box inside. He then went over to reexamine the message scratched on the wall.

"I wish I'd listened to Mr. Enright that night," I said. "He wanted to tell me something, and I wouldn't take the time to listen. If I had, both he and Bill Trelawney might still be alive."

"You don't know that. Timothy was separated. Maybe he wanted to tell you he thinks you're cute."

I scoffed as I tilted my head up at him. "You don't seriously believe that, do you?"

"That you're cute? Sure, I do." He gave

me a half grin.

I rolled my eyes.

"Okay," he said. "I seriously doubt Timothy Enright wanted to ask you out on a date. He had to have been head over heels for Lorraine in order to put up with her for as long as he did."

"Do you know her? Lorraine?"

"Barely. I did know Tim fairly well, and I know that woman gave him a ton of grief."

"In what way?" I pulled the storeroom door shut and walked slowly to the sitting area. "Someone mentioned she'd been after Mr. Enright to move his business for quite a while." I sat down on one of the red chairs, while Detective Nash took a seat on one of the navy sofas.

He picked up a pillow and ran a hand over the Colonial knots making up the candlewick design. "That was only part of it. It seemed she was never satisfied. She'd come into the store and have a tantrum right there in front of everyone, because she wanted some piece of jewelry or furniture they couldn't afford."

"How embarrassing for Mr. Enright and his customers."

Detective Nash nodded. "It was. I have an ex-wife, and we never had blowups like that. Of course, it was only Lorraine blowing up.

Tim always tried to quietly placate her."

"I've only met Mrs. Enright a couple of times," I said, "but she isn't quiet."

"If anyone drove Timothy Enright to an early grave, it was her." He traced the pillow's design with his index finger. "But I didn't say that."

"Do you think Lorraine Enright might've poisoned her husband?" I asked.

"I didn't say that, either. Everyone is still a suspect at this point, Ms. Singer. Even you."

"Ah, now, there's the Detective Nash I've come to know."

The bell above the door jingled, heralding Sadie's arrival. She greeted Angus and then stopped short at the sight of Detective Nash sitting on the sofa.

"Ted, what are you doing here? I thought it was your day off."

"It is." He put the pillow aside. "I'm just here seeing if Ms. Singer had any additional information . . . seeing if we can add any more pieces to this puzzle."

"Uh-huh." Sadie crossed her arms and walked around to the other red chair.

"Hopefully, Sadie and I will have more information to report tomorrow evening. We're going —"

Sadie collapsed into a coughing fit. I

waited until she was finished before continuing.

"We're going to the prison to see Norman Patrick."

Detective Nash looked from me to Sadie — who was now covering her eyes with her hand — and back to me. "You're what?"

"Going to talk with Norm Patrick. It was Sadie's idea. She said he likes blondes."

Again, Detective Nash looked back and forth from me to Sadie, his mouth gaping open.

"I know it sounds like a harebrained idea," I said. "I thought so, too, at first. But I'm going to ask Mr. Patrick if Timothy Enright had anything to do with Four Square Development."

"And, of course, he'll open right up and tell you," Detective Nash said. "Will you be carrying sodium pentothal in your gigantic yellow purse?" He raised his eyes to the ceiling. "Oh, wait . . . it won't matter. The guard who checks your gigantic yellow purse and makes you walk through a metal detector will confiscate it." He smirked.

It was that smirk that sent me over the edge. I leaned forward and licked my lips. "What makes you think I'll need truth serum?" I asked in a hushed, sexy voice.

"You c-can't go into a prison and . . .

117

be . . . seductive!" Detective Nash practically yelled. "Are you out of your mind?"

I snapped my fingers, and Angus trotted over to sit by my side. I scratched his head. "I'm going to get to the truth about all this. I've worked too hard to let a shadow hang over this shop — or over me."

CHAPTER SIX

Later that afternoon, I was unpacking the Halloween products that had arrived that morning. The scarecrow designs were adorable. There were also cross-stitch cards with characters and sayings. A cross-eyed bat was combined with the phrase "You drive me batty." A mummy said, "I'm all wrapped up in you." A black cat declared the card's recipient "purrrfect." Yeah, corny; I know. But the cards really were cute. And if I got a card like one of these, I would adore it. How nice it would be to know someone thought enough to actually make me something, especially for Halloween.

There was the most adorable haunted-house project. Darling little ghosts peeped out of the windows, and a black cat sat on the porch. Of course, a full moon loomed overhead, with a bat flying nearby. Two tombstones stood by a bare-limbed tree. The tombstones had names and little epitaphs: *I told you I was sick!* and *Ima Goner.* There were other suggestions on the back: *Myra Mains, Emma Ghost, Will Knott Rest,* and *Yul B. Next.* I absolutely had to have one of these haunted houses of my own, and promised myself I'd start it as soon as I finished my tote bag. Okay, or the MacKenzies' Mochas logo. What can I say? I like to multitask.

I heard the bell over the door jingle and called, "I'll be right there!"

"That's all right," Sadie said. "I'll come to you. What are you doing?"

"Getting ready to stock these Halloween kits."

Sadie picked up a kit depicting a teddy bear wearing a pumpkin costume. "How sweet!"

"Do you want it? I owe you after all the free coffees you've given me."

"Do you think I could do it?" Sadie turned the kit over to read the back. "It looks a little hard."

"You totally could. Have you ever done needlepoint?"

"No."

"I'll teach you. It's easy, and it goes really fast."

"Good. I like fast." Sadie gave me a pointed look. "At least, I *usually* like fast.

What was with you making eyes at Ted Nash today?"

"I did *not* make eyes at Ted Nash. I merely wiped that arrogant smirk off his face."

"Well, you certainly did that. But I think you might've melted his shoes, too."

I laughed. "No, I did not."

"I, uh . . . thought you liked Todd."

"I do like Todd."

"And?" Sadie prompted.

"And what?"

"What was Ted Nash doing here on his day off?"

I shrugged. "He called me last night and asked if he could come by. He said he said he wanted to take another look around."

"On his day off."

"I hadn't realized it was his day off. But I'm serious, Sadie, I want to get to the truth about this whole Enright/Trelawney/Four Square thing."

"I get that, but —"

"But what?" I put my hands on my hips.

"There appeared to be some serious sparks flying between you and Ted today, that's all."

"He's investigating me for murder. That's such a turn-on."

"It's just that Todd likes you, and —"

"And what? I'm acting like a tramp? I'm

sorry. Please pass my apologies along to whomever else you think needs one."

"I'm not accusing you of anything, Marcy. I'm just saying that if Todd likes you and you like Detective Nash, I'd appreciate your not leading Todd on."

I went back to my box of embroidery kits. "I need to get these put up. I'll see you tomorrow when I get back from the prison."

"Oh, so now Blake, Todd, and I aren't going?"

"Why would you want to? I might lead Todd on."

Sadie huffed, pitched her bear pattern back into the box, and left.

I finished putting up the kits. I did like Todd, but he and I had not even been on an official date. It's hard to get to know someone when you're usually part of a four-some or — in the case of the grand-opening party — a crowd. And there was something a little exciting about wiping that smirk off Ted Nash's haughty face . . . the way his full lips parted slightly when I leaned closer to him, the way his eyes darkened, the way he caught and held his breath. It was a powerful feeling. Maybe I did like him a micro bit. Maybe not having had a date in more than a year was getting to me. Maybe I should "get thee to a nunnery."

I blew out a breath and looked down at Angus, who was lying on his bed. He looked up at me without raising his head. He was so adorable when he did that. I bent and kissed the top of his head.

"I'd never go to a nunnery without you, Angus."

"I hope you don't go to a nunnery at all."

I stood so quickly, I nearly fell. "Hey, Todd. I didn't hear the bell."

"No wonder. It seems your thoughts were a million miles away."

"Not a million, but they were wandering."

"To a nunnery, no less." He grinned.

I bit my lower lip. "Long story. Sometimes I'd like to simply run away and disappear."

"One of those days, huh?"

I nodded. "Sadie and I had an argument."

"Have you made up yet?"

I shook my head.

He looked at his watch. "It's nearly closing time. Come on."

I looked down at the almost-empty box.

"It can wait until Monday, can't it?" He cocked his head and looked at me with those milk-chocolate eyes. "Please?" He smiled. "I was looking forward to the four of us going to the prison tomorrow."

I laughed. "Yeah, it's not every day you get to do that." I put the box into the storeroom, grabbed one of the teddy bear pumpkin kits off the shelf, and began shutting off the lights. "Come on, Angus."

I turned the OPEN sign to CLOSED and locked the door behind us. As we were walking next door to MacKenzies' Mochas, Sadie stepped out and started toward us.

"I was coming to apologize," she said.

"Me, too."

We hugged.

"So, we're still on for tomorrow?" Todd asked.

"Oh, heck, yeah," Sadie said. "Nobody's going on a prison road trip without me."

What does one wear to a prison? I asked myself, my inner voice reminding me of Lovey Howell from *Gilligan's Island.* As I looked through my closet, Angus lay on the floor, chewing an eco-friendly bone that was supposed to make his breath smell minty. I hadn't yet broken the news to him that he couldn't join me on my field trip to the prison and that he'd have to stay in the backyard all day. Don't get me wrong; Angus loves his little fenced-off piece of real estate, and he especially enjoys lounging on the back porch swing. He has plenty of food, water, and toys out there to keep him occupied. It's just the way he looks at me when he knows I'm going somewhere without him. Guilt, guilt, guilt.

I turned my attention back to the closet. If only I had an orange jumpsuit . . . or maybe an orange minidress like that girl on *Pushing Daisies* wore. No. It would be my luck for them to throw me in jail for contempt or something.

I opted for a floral-print skirt, pink V-neck sweater, and taupe platform pumps. I curled my hair, which makes me — in my opinion — look more polished and professional. I usually let it do whatever it wants, and it looks kinda wild. I like it, though; it's fun and funky, casual and relaxed. I did a quick scalp check — no sign of roots yet. Roots suck. They tell everybody who's thinking *That couldn't possibly be her natural hair color* that they're right. When really it's none of their business in the first place that my hair is naturally a dull, mousy brown.

I sat down at the vanity to put on my makeup. "What do you think, Angus? Should I take Mr. Patrick a box of candy? Is that sort of thing allowed?" I turned to look at him, but he completely ignored me. He knew something was up. It was the hair. I should've explained things to him before I curled my hair.

I was putting on my lipstick when the

doorbell rang.

"Coming!" I checked the clock. They were early.

When I opened the door, I was surprised to find Ted Nash there. He was back in his suit, with his badge clipped to his belt. "Good afternoon, Ms. Singer. May I come in?"

"Of course."

He noticed me looking at the street beyond him. "You're expecting someone?"

I nodded. "We're going to the prison today."

"Oh, that's right. I honestly think you should reconsider that. It's not a wise decision. And if Chief Myers finds out, he'll be livid. He hates it when civilians interfere with our work."

"What brings you by?" I asked.

"Bill Trelawney was killed by a .38-caliber slug. Would you happen to own a gun, Ms. Singer?"

"No, I don't, but I'll happily submit to a search."

His lips twitched. "I can look at you and fairly conclusively ascertain you're not concealing a weapon."

"I meant the house. Feel free to search the house for any sort of . . . artillery."

"Not necessary."

Blake's van pulled into the driveway beside the detective's black cruiser.

"Looks like your ride's here," Detective Nash said. "If you insist on following through with this, be careful, all right?"

"I will."

He turned and waved in the direction of Blake's van and got into his car. I held up one finger to let Blake know I'd be there in a minute. As I went to the kitchen for Angus' provisions, Sadie came inside.

"Need help with anything?" she asked.

"No. I'm gathering up a few things to keep Angus busy today, that's all." I knew her real question was why Detective Nash had been here, but I was still miffed enough about yesterday not to tell her.

I filled Angus' food and water bowls, and I put his teddy bear on the porch swing. He had other toys out there already. I called him, and he came moping into the kitchen.

"I'm sorry," I told him. "It's only for a while." I could've sworn I heard Glenn Frey singing about my lyin' eyes.

I opened the back door. Angus took his bone and went out onto the porch, giving me an admonishing glance over his shoulder before I closed the door.

Honey, you can't hide your lyin' eyes.

"Shut up, Glenn," I muttered.

127

"What?" Sadie asked. She was nearly bursting with wanting to ask why Detective Nash had been here. I could read it all over her face.

I smiled. "I'm ready."

Sadie and I went out and got into Blake's cream-colored van, which bore the Mac-Kenzies' Mochas logo on both sides. I was in the back with Todd.

"Hello there, Marcy," he said, grinning. "You look sensational."

"Thank you very much."

"When we got here, I was afraid I might have to engage Ted Nash in fisticuffs."

"Fisticuffs?" I giggled.

"Yeah. I thought maybe he was trying to haul you away."

"Wouldn't that be ironic?" I asked. "Getting all dressed up to go visit a jail and getting dragged in for real? Lucky for me, I don't own a gun."

Sadie leaned around her seat to look at me. "You mean, he came to ask if you own a gun?"

"Yeah. I even told him to search the house if he wanted to. I don't have a .38. Do you guys know anyone who does?"

"We do," Blake said. "I keep it in the safe at the shop."

"What?" I asked. "Why?"

"Any number of reasons. Bears, for one thing. I mean, it isn't often they come into town, and I would hate to have to shoot one. But I'd protect Sadie, myself, and our staff if I needed to."

I had a feeling he wasn't talking about bears exclusively now.

"I have a .38 I keep locked up at the pub," Todd said. "Why was Ted so interested in a .38, anyway? Lots of people have them."

"He said that was the kind of gun used to kill Bill Trelawney."

The prison was big. It was clean, too, and had a hospital-like, industrial-clean odor. It wasn't that I had been expecting the prison to be dumpy and dirty, but I simply hadn't thought it would be as big or as clean as it was in actuality. And the acoustics! Blake sneezed when we first walked in, and it echoed as if we were in a canyon.

Guards wearing blue latex gloves went through Sadie's and my purses and had the men empty their pockets. Then our belongings were sent through the X-ray machine as we individually passed through the metal detector. We were given the okay to venture on ahead.

A guard sitting behind a podium beyond the security checkpoint stood and unlocked the doors leading to the visitor's information desk. He then closed the doors behind us, and I could hear his key turning the tumbler in the lock.

I tried to remind myself that this was a minimum-security, rather than a maximum-security, prison, but somehow that reminder — combined with the fact that I was now locked up inside this facility — didn't bring me much comfort.

The visitor's information desk was basically a large steel countertop. Guards checked our driver's licenses, presumably to make sure we weren't wanted for anything. We were then asked to state the reason for our visit.

"We'd like to speak with Mr. Norman Patrick," I said.

"Is Mr. Patrick expecting you?" one of the guards asked.

"No."

The guard radioed someone else and told this person to see if Mr. Patrick would agree to see Marcella Singer, Sadie MacKenzie, Blake MacKenzie, and Todd Calloway. While we waited for an answer, I wondered if we'd completely wasted a trip.

Within a few minutes, the guard's radio crackled and a voice said, "Patrick said to send them back."

I was pondering if that meant "back home" or "back to where Mr. Patrick is waiting" when the guard instructed us to sign the logbook and to once again indicate the purpose of our visit. After we did that, the guard opened a set of doors and led us down a hallway to what amounted to a snack bar. The room was filled with vending machines and small round tables and chairs bolted to the floor. I fleetingly wondered why there were no pictures of any kind in the hallways or common areas.

Our guard nodded to one of the other guards stationed throughout the snack bar, and then he left us. There were a handful of other inmates sitting at the tables. Two sat alone, another two sat together, and the other three had visitors.

Sadie and Blake were already acquainted with Mr. Patrick through the coffee shop. They strode over to the beefy man with square-rimmed glasses and a ready smile. Todd and I followed. I recognized him from the photos I'd seen in Riley Kendall's office.

"Sadie MacKenzie," he said. "You're looking as lovely as ever."

"Thank you so much, Mr. Patrick."

"I'm afraid the coffee in this place is nowhere near the caliber of yours."

131

"When you get home, come by the shop for a cup on the house," Blake said.

"I'll take you up on that," Mr. Patrick said. He squinted past Sadie. "This pretty little sprite must be Marcella Singer."

"Marcy," I said, holding out my hand. "Please, call me Marcy."

"Pull up a chair, Marcy," he said.

"I'm afraid I can't, sir. They're bolted to the floor."

Mr. Patrick laughed and slapped his thigh. "What a peach."

I did sit down across from him. Sadie took another available chair.

"I'm Todd Calloway." Todd reached across the table to shake Mr. Patrick's hand. "I own the Brew Crew. It's on the other side of the street from MacKenzies' Mochas."

"Don't know that I've ever been there," Mr. Patrick said. "But it's nice to meet you." He turned his attention back to me. "To what do I owe this honor?"

Blake and Todd sat at the table beside us, since there were only four chairs at Mr. Patrick's table.

I leaned forward. "I'm here to ask you about Timothy Enright. Did you know him?"

"Sure did."

"I suppose you heard he died in the

storeroom of my shop."

Mr. Patrick nodded. "Riley told me about it. Brought me the newspaper, too. I hate that for Tim. I really do."

"So do I." I bit my lower lip. "His wife thinks I somehow did him in."

"You, Little Bit?" Mr. Patrick laughed. "Why, you couldn't hurt a fly. You remind me of Tinkerbell."

I joined in his laughter. "I'm only sorry I can't muster up some fairy dust and fly away from Lorraine Enright. She hates me!"

"I don't doubt that. There aren't many people Lorraine Enright does like, and that included her husband." He reached out and took one of my hands in both of his. "She won't be happy when that will is read."

"Why won't she be happy with the will?" Sadie asked.

"You'll have to take my word on that one. Attorney-client privilege and all that. Let's just say she won't be shopping at Saks."

"But that's a given, isn't it?" I asked. "Mrs. Enright said her husband went bankrupt because Mr. Trelawney wanted to bring in new businesses . . . like mine."

Mr. Patrick grinned. "Tim didn't go bankrupt."

He still held my hand, so I felt entitled to ask him whatever I wanted. "Was Mr. Enright involved with Four Square Development?"

He made a sucking noise. "Why do you ask?"

"Because he scratched *four square fifth w* on my storeroom wall before he died."

His mouth spread into a wide smile, and he suddenly reminded me of the shark Bruce in *Finding Nemo.* "Hard to say, Tinkerbell. But it's probably best you leave all this alone. Concentrate on your shop. How's that going? Doing well?"

"Very well, thank you," I said.

"I'm glad." His hands tightened on mine. "You don't need to go around stirring up hornets' nests."

"But I do, Mr. Patrick. I'm apparently a suspect in the murders of both Timothy Enright and Bill Trelawney. I have to find out who killed them, or else I might be next."

"Not if you stay away from hornets' nests."

"Why do you keep saying that?" I asked.

Mr. Patrick sighed, and his breath wasn't pleasant. "Look, you seem like a nice kid. I was sorry to hear about Enright. He was a decent guy, and, truth be told, when I found out the cops thought he was murdered, I figured it was his wife. When I heard about Bill Trelawney being shot in the head, that shook me up." He released my hand to swipe a bead of sweat off his upper lip.

"Can I get you some water or something?" I asked.

He shook his head. "Bill Trelawney was involved with Four Square Development and was working with someone, but he was the only one who knew who it was. Whoever it was, the person always worked behind the scenes and was careful to operate solely through Trelawney."

"Then how did Mr. Trelawney avoid prosecution?"

"I don't know," Mr. Patrick said. "I only know his partner was someone powerful . . . someone able to make sure the two of them got off scot-free."

"But from what you're telling me, you could've told the authorities what you know about Mr. Trelawney and had him arrested, too. They might have even cut you a deal," I said.

He chuckled. "You watch too much television. I didn't give Bill up to the feds because they hadn't found everything." He glanced around the room before lowering his voice. "They thought they had, and that was good enough for the others and me. But now that he's dead . . ." He shook his head. "There's a loose cannon out there,

135

and I have no idea who it is . . . and what he might do next."

CHAPTER SEVEN

My head was spinning when we left the prison. I felt literally light-headed — like given half the chance, my head might float away like a balloon. I'm not sure whether it was from Norman Patrick's death grip on my hand, the nauseating odor of industrial cleansers, the feeling of claustrophobia emanating from the prisoners, or the information Mr. Patrick simultaneously gave and withheld.

As soon as we got into Blake's van, I dug around in my purse and found my hand sanitizer. I squirted a generous amount onto my palm. "Anyone else?"

Sadie was quick to accept my offer. She then handed the sanitizer to Blake. Todd took some, too, though I got the feeling it was mostly to avoid being the odd man out. Of course, it wasn't his hand encased between Norman Patrick's sweaty palms for so long. I suppressed a shudder, returned the hand sanitizer to my purse, and melted into the seat. If I wasn't afraid I'd drool or snore in front of Todd, I'd have let myself drift off to sleep. Long car rides do that to me when I'm not driving.

"I've got an idea," Todd said. "When we go through Lincoln City, let's stop at that great ocean-view restaurant for lunch. On me."

"You mean Carillo's?" Blake asked.

"That's the one."

"Oooh, I love that place," Sadie said. "They make the best crab cakes."

I didn't hear another word until we stopped in Carillo's parking lot.

"Marcy," Todd said softly. "We're here."

I opened my eyes and saw light blue denim. It was the front of Todd's shirt. My head was nestled against his shoulder.

I raised my head and looked into his handsome, tenderly smiling face. "I'm so sorry. I . . . I didn't mean —"

"It's okay. I know you're not the type of girl who sleeps around." He chuckled as I blushed. "You've been through a lot these past few days. I'm glad I was here to provide a shoulder."

And I was glad Blake and Sadie had already gone into the restaurant. I gave Todd an awkward smile and retrieved my purse. He removed his arm from around me as I took a compact out my makeup bag. My mascara had smudged, but otherwise, I didn't look as bad as I'd feared. I swiped away the smudges with a makeup sponge, smoothed my hair, and put on a fresh coat of lipstick.

"Ready?" he asked.

I nodded. A surreptitious glance assured me there were no drool spots or makeup stains on Todd's shirt. That was a relief. As for the snoring, I'd have to check with Sadie on that one.

We walked into the restaurant, and Sadie waved us over to the table.

"What a marvelous view," I said.

"Isn't it, though?" Blake gave me a sidelong glance. "Are you going to be able to stay awake through lunch? They're not very busy right now, so we should be served fairly quickly and —"

"Quit that," Sadie said. She turned to me. "He loves to mess with you so much, I'd almost believe you were his sister." She frowned. "Has this mess been keeping you awake nights? Oh, what am I saying? Of course it has. How could it not?"

"Hey, look." Todd nodded toward the window.

I gasped. "How sweet!"

A seal had risen out of the water not far from shore. I could even make out the black spots on its body. The seal did a sort of backflip and swam away. But even after the others began perusing their menus, I kept watching in the hope I'd see it again.

Suddenly, just beyond a red buoy, I saw what appeared to be a burst of steam rising several feet above the ocean. "What on earth . . . ?"

"What's wrong?" Sadie asked.

I described what I'd seen. Sadie, Blake, and Todd smiled at each other and then at me.

"Keep watching," Todd said.

In less than a minute, there was another burst of steam or water or *something.* This one was several feet in front of where the first one had occurred.

I shook my head. "What is that?"

"It's a gray whale," Blake said. "What you're seeing is its spout . . . a cloud of moisture it shoots into the air."

"Wow. That's cool."

And then, just like that, I saw its tail flip up out of the ocean. I clapped my hands together. "Did you see that?"

"Uh-huh," Todd said. "It's diving for food now. That dive helps propel the whale toward the bottom of the ocean, where it can feed." He pointed to the smooth circle of water left in the wake of the whale's tail. "See that? It's called a fluke print."

"A what?"

"A fluke print," he repeated. "The two lobes of the whale's tail are called the fluke."

"How do you guys know so much about whales?" I asked.

"Every year a bunch of us go to Depoe Bay for the winter and spring migratory whale watch," Sadie said. "The winter watch week is between Christmas and New Year's Day. The gray whales migrate from the Arctic Ocean to Mexico so the moms can have their calves in the warm bays."

"We'll take you this year if you'd like to go," Blake said.

"I'd love to."

The waiter arrived, forcing me to turn my attention away from the ocean and consult my menu while everyone else was ordering. In the end, I decided on a chef's salad and a small bowl of tomato bisque.

The waiter left to get our drink orders.

"Have you talked with your mom lately?" Sadie asked.

I smiled. "I talked to her Friday night. She's doing great, although she did mention one diva on the set."

"Let me guess." Sadie grinned. "She

141

doesn't even have a starring role."

We laughed.

I turned to Todd. "My mom is a costume designer. She's currently on location in New York. Sadie has heard about Mom and her antics since we were roommates in college, so she knows all about Mom's 'divas.' "

"The 'divas' are always actresses with small roles," Sadie said. "The stars usually know better."

"That's right," I said. "I can only remember one actress with a starring role who acted haughty toward Mom."

"And she appeared on set in a garment that made everybody — paparazzi included — speculate about her 'belly bump.' "

Sadie and I were still laughing when the waiter returned with our drinks. Todd and Blake merely sat there with bemused smiles on their faces. We thanked the waiter, and then I picked up the thread of the story.

"See, Mom has been doing this for a long time. She's highly sought after and is something of a diva herself."

"Oh yes," Sadie said. "If anybody gives Beverly Singer too hard a time, she walks."

"And then whoever made that happen has the entire production staff unhappy with them." I took a sip of my water. "Nobody wants anything to happen that's going to delay the production schedule, and replacing a costume designer —"

"Especially one the caliber of Marcy's mom," Sadie interjected.

"— can throw them off for weeks." The guys still looked clueless. I was about to try to steer the conversation to something that would be of more interest to them when Sadie spoke again.

"Did you tell her what's going on?"

"A little. She knows about Mr. Enright turning up dead in the storeroom, but she doesn't know about Mr. Trelawney. I thought it best not to worry her. After all, what could she do? She and I are on opposite sides of the country."

"You've got a point." Sadie unfolded her napkin and began smoothing it out. "And it's not like you're alone here. You know you've got Blake and me. We'll be there for you anytime."

"So will I," Todd said.

"Thank you," I said. "That means a lot. Somehow, though, I think I'd feel better if everyone — including prison inmates — would stop telling me to be careful."

"So, how's business going?" Blake asked. "I heard you tell Mr. Patrick that you were doing well."

"I am. The first day — my first customer,

actually — a lady named Sarah Crenshaw came in and bought several things for a project she's doing for her granddaughter. She signed up for my crewel class, and some of her friends called to sign up, as well. They'll practically make up my entire crewel class."

"I know Mrs. Crenshaw," Sadie said. "She comes into the shop a lot." She turned to Blake. "She's always nicely dressed, elegant, refined. . . ."

Blake nodded. "Orders the caramel latte made with nonfat milk."

"That's her."

"I really am so pleased with the number of students signed up for classes," I said. "Not only because of the business they'll be bringing in, but because it's such a wonderful way to get to know the people of Tallulah Falls."

"Just keep in mind," Todd said, "some of us folks are nicer than others."

"Duly noted." I laughed, but something about his lighthearted comment lingered.

That evening, I was lounging on the sofa in black track pants and a white T-shirt, reading an Audrey Hepburn biography. Angus was snoozing on the floor by my side. About every other page, I'd think, *Wow, she was classy. I wish I could be like that.*

My mom is Audrey-classy. She can walk into a room, and everyone turns to look at her . . . not so much because of her appearance, but because of her essence.

One of my favorite Audrey Hepburn quotes, and believe me I have a few, is "For beautiful eyes, look for the good in others; for beautiful lips, speak only words of kindness; and for poise, walk with the knowledge that you are never alone."

Isn't that terrific?

The doorbell rang. I tried to glide over the carpet Audrey style, but stubbed my toe. Oh, well. We'd have shared a laugh at that, though. Audrey loved to laugh.

I opened the door and was delighted to see Reggie and a man who must surely be Manu standing at her side. Reggie was wearing her usual Indian-inspired tunic and slacks, while Manu was dressed in jeans, cowboy boots, and a red and black flannel shirt.

"Hi!" I gave Reggie a quick hug. We hadn't known each other long, but there was something so appealing and wise about her, it felt like we were old friends.

"I hope we're not interrupting anything," she said. "We were in the area. I knew this was your house because I was friends with the Wilsons." The Wilsons were the previous owners, who had decamped for California. Sometimes I couldn't say I blamed them.

"Not at all. Please come in."

She introduced me to Manu. Besides being dressed in a more traditionally Western style than Reggie, Manu had a short, stocky build and heavy-lidded, intelligent eyes.

"Let me put Angus outside," I said.

"Don't you dare," Reggie said, sitting on a chair in the living room. "Come here, baby."

Angus happily trotted over to sit beside Reggie's chair.

"She's animal crazy," Manu said.

"So am I. Can I get you something to drink?"

Both declined my offer, and Manu and I sat down on opposite sides of the sofa.

"I told Manu about the trip you planned to take today," Reggie said. "We decided to stop by to see if you went."

I nodded. "We went. And I asked Mr. Patrick about Timothy Enright. He didn't tell me much. He said he knew Mr. Enright and that he'd prepared his will. And he indicated that Mr. Enright hadn't gone bankrupt. I wonder why Lorraine thought he had."

"You know, you really should leave the

investigating to the professionals. You don't want to put yourself in harm's way like that." Manu drummed his fingertips on the arm of the sofa. "But this does set me to thinking. Maybe Tim was hiding his money from Lorraine. They were going through a divorce, after all. Did Patrick confirm any involvement by Enright in Four Square Development?"

"Did you expect him to?" Reggie asked her husband.

"I did," I said. "I mean, he's in prison, and Timothy Enright is dead. What has Mr. Patrick got to lose?"

"Good point," Manu said. "What else *could* he have to lose?"

I shook my head. "I'm not following you."

"There are only two reasons Norman Patrick wouldn't confirm Timothy Enright's involvement in Four Square Development. One, Enright had no involvement. Or two, Enright's involvement came after he was put away, and he didn't know about it."

"You believe the investigation was incomplete?" I asked.

"I do," Manu said. "I believe the investigators only uncovered the tip of the iceberg. They didn't dig deeply enough below the surface."

"Manu has always believed the auditors

couldn't get sufficient evidence to prove everything they suspected," Reggie said. "So they only got warrants on those things they could win convictions on."

"What else did the auditors think was going on?" I asked.

Manu shook his head. "No one at our department knows. It was a federal case, and we were kept out of the loop. We can only speculate."

"Did Norman say anything else?" Reggie asked.

"He told me Bill Trelawney had been involved with Four Square Development's operations, but that he'd worked with someone else."

Manu *hmmph*ed, indicating he wasn't truly surprised about Bill Trelawney. Clearly, the Four Square case was a whole lot more complicated than most people knew. "Who was this other person?" Manu asked.

"Only Bill knew. Mr. Patrick seemed to think he was pretty powerful, though. I think he's scared, Manu." And, truth be told, so was I.

Monday morning, I was sitting at the counter, playing blackjack with Jill (she was winning, by the way) when Vera Langhorne came in. I scooped up the cards.

"Morning, Vera. I got some really cute Halloween merchandise in over the weekend."

"I'll give it a look-see in a few minutes." She went over to the sitting area and took her cross-stitch project from her tote. The work she had done so far was actually beginning to look like a teacup.

"Mind if I join you?" I asked.

"I was hoping you would. If you don't mind my saying so, you looked a mite lonely when I came in. Where's Angus?"

"Todd Calloway came by and asked to take him for a walk on the beach."

"That was nice." She grinned. "Seems Detective Nash isn't the only eligible bachelor in Tallulah Falls setting his cap for the new girl."

I curled up in the red chair with my own project. "I highly doubt either of them has set his cap for me." I began to count and stitch.

"If you say so. I've been married for thirty-three years, but I can still tell when a young man is interested in a young woman." She looked up from her work. "And if you can't, you might consider playing cards with your mannequin less and watching more reality television."

I laughed. "You're in a punchy mood. You must've had an interesting weekend."

"I had a delightful weekend, thank you. John was ever so complimentary. He was interested in the tote bag I'm making, he bragged on dinner, he told me I'm looking fantastic. . . ." She smiled. "I think finding a creative outlet has been good for me. For us."

"I'm glad."

"And what did you do this weekend?"

I silently debated on how much to tell her. She had been the one to clue me in on Four Square Development, but could I trust her? Vera did like to talk, and I wasn't sure I wanted all of Tallulah Falls knowing I'd gone to the prison to see Norman Patrick on Sunday.

"I worked on Saturday and had lunch with Todd, Sadie, and Blake on Sunday." That was true enough. "I wish this ordeal with Mr. Enright — and now Bill Trelawney — was resolved. It's so upsetting."

"I know. Poor Margaret. And now with that drill sergeant Sylvia besieging the house, she must be even more miserable."

"Isn't that the truth? How about Lorraine Enright?" I asked. "How does she appear to be coping?"

"I don't know that Lorraine is all that

broken up over Tim."

"From what little I've seen of her, she seems more angry than anything. Of course, isn't anger one of the first stages of grief?"

"Maybe," Vera said, "but she appears to be more concerned about her finances than her bereavement. I went by the bank Saturday morning to take John a muffin I'd bought him at Sadie's place, and Lorraine nearly plowed me over coming out of John's office. I asked him who'd put a burr under her saddle, and he said she was angry that there was so little money in her and Tim's joint accounts."

Hmmm. I wondered if that was something her husband should have repeated. "Do you think Tim had taken some of their money without telling her?"

"I don't know, but it would serve her right if he did. Lorraine always has been greedy." She checked her instructions. "It says here I'm supposed to make a half stitch. How do I do that?"

I moved over to the sofa to demonstrate a half stitch, and wondered what Timothy Enright had done with his and Lorraine's money. I showed Vera how to make the half stitch by coming only halfway to the next point and placing the other half of the cross-stitch normally.

The phone rang. I'd forgotten to bring the cordless phone over, so I hurried to the counter to answer it.

"Can't Jill get that?" Vera joked.

"Nope. She refuses to answer the phone, dust, or clean windows, but she does work cheap." I picked up the phone. "Good morning. The Seven-Year Stitch."

I was surprised — I'd almost go as far as to say *shocked* — to hear Riley Kendall's voice.

"Good morning, Marcy. How are you?"

"I'm fine, thank you. How are you?"

"I'm a smidge troubled that you and I got started off on such a sour note. I'd like to remedy that by buying you lunch today."

"I certainly appreciate the offer, Ms. Kendall, but I can't close the shop during the day."

"I anticipated that . . . and, please, call me Riley. I'll bring my mom along to watch your shop, and we can have lunch next door at MacKenzies' Mochas."

"Won't that be a huge imposition on your mom?"

"Of course not. She's happy to help. See you at noon, then?"

"Yes, I . . . I'll be looking forward to it."

When I turned the phone off and returned to the sitting area, Vera had placed her

152

project in her lap and was looking at me with unabashed curiosity.

"Did I hear right?" she asked. "Are Riley Kendall and her mother on their way over here?"

"Not until noon. Why?"

Vera grimaced. "Let's just say I'm one of the last people Camille Patrick — Riley's mother — wants to run into." She checked her watch. "I still have an hour, but I'll leave in forty minutes to be on the safe side."

I decided Vera's nosiness about my phone call entitled me to a little nosiness of my own. "Why are there bad feelings between you and Mrs. Patrick?"

"Her husband fancied himself a womanizer back before . . . well, before he went to jail. He was involved in that Four Square Development mess I told you about. So a little over a year ago, we were at a party, and she overheard her husband making an advance toward me. I quickly put him in his place and forgot about it until one of my friends called me the next day and asked if it was true that I'd tried to seduce Norman Patrick."

"How did you get blamed?"

"I have no idea. Camille heard him. She knew precisely what had happened and that I was not at fault."

"My question is, why would she advertise it at all? I mean, no matter whom she felt was at fault, why would she want to spread gossip about it?"

"This all happened right before everything went down about Four Square. Camille nearly went crazy defending her husband over anything and everything. But in the end, he was still found guilty."

The bell over the door jingled, and Vera froze midstitch.

CHAPTER EIGHT

Luckily, it was only Todd bringing Angus back.

Angus greeted me enthusiastically. I smiled up at Todd. "Did you guys have fun?"

"A blast," Todd said. "We even saw a puffin."

My eyes widened. "He didn't —"

"Angus was a perfect gentleman."

"I hope he will be for Mrs. Patrick."

This time Todd's eyes widened in surprise.

"Riley Kendall called out of the blue and asked me to lunch. She said her mother would babysit the store. I'm not sure she knows about Angus." I took Todd's arm and propelled him toward the door. "I'll stop in at the Brew Crew on my way home and tell you all about it."

"Okay, but I don't mind keeping Angus for a while longer if you need me to."

"Thanks, anyway, but I'm sure he'll be okay. See you later."

Todd looked confused as he left . . . and maybe even a little hurt. But I'd explain everything to him this evening.

When Todd left, I returned to the red chair, Vera, and my cross-stitch project.

"You sure gave him the bum's rush," Vera said. "Did he do something to blow his chances with you at lunch yesterday?"

"Not at all. But I know Riley is coming and that you might need my help again before you leave. Those half stitches can be tricky. Besides, I know Todd has more important things to do today than keep an eye on Angus."

"I don't know. He seemed put out to me."

The door opened and Vera gave me a smug smile, as if she expected Todd to come storming back in for the two of us to have a Rhett and Scarlett moment.

You need to be kissed, Marcy . . . often . . . and by someone who knows how.

The smile slipped away when Vera realized that, instead of Todd, Riley Kendall and Camille Patrick had walked in.

I stood. "Hi, there. I really hate imposing on your mother like this. We could order our food from MacKenzies' Mochas, and I could run next door to pick it up when it's ready."

"Nonsense," Camille said. "You two run

along and enjoy your lunch . . . unless you don't trust me with your shop."

"Oh, no, it's not that." Although it was a little *that.* "I just hate to bother you. Besides, you need to have lunch, too, Mrs. Patrick."

"I've already eaten. But thank you anyway."

Defeated, I gave in. Besides, Riley Kendall had to have an excellent reason for so adamantly wanting to have lunch with me, and I needed to find out what that reason was. "I wasn't expecting you this early. Let me tidy up, and I'll be right with you."

I began gathering my embroidery supplies. Vera followed suit.

"I realize we're terribly early," Riley said, "but I thought that since time seems to be an issue for you today, we'd eat early and avoid the lunch rush."

"That's fine," I said.

"Vera." The contempt-laden word was uttered by Camille Patrick. I stiffened.

"Camille," Vera said.

"I didn't realize you were a stitcher," Camille said.

"I've only just begun."

White lace and promises. Lovely. Now Karen Carpenter's voice would haunt me the rest of the day.

"John loves it," Vera continued. "He enjoys

my creativity."

"I somehow doubt he's the only one," Camille said.

I felt I had to intervene. A catfight between these two could completely destroy my shop. A flash of Vera and Camille snarling at each other while wielding sewing scissors like two samurai warriors while yarn, thread, and patterns died painful deaths plowed through my mind and left a dull throbbing behind my right eye.

"Vera's doing really great," I said. "All my students are. We're currently making tote bags in the cross-stitch class."

Vera and Camille still glared malevolently at each other.

Riley clapped her hands twice. "Ladies, draw in your claws. We don't have time for this. Marcy and I need to get next door, and I know she doesn't want to leave her store with this sort of nonsense going on."

"I was just leaving," Vera said.

"Good." Riley headed for the door. "We'll walk you out."

"Thank you for watching the store, Mrs. Patrick," I said. I showed her how to ring up a purchase on the cash register, though it wasn't extremely likely I'd miss a customer as long as we kept lunch fairly brief. "I think everything else is pretty self-explanatory, but if you need anything, I have business cards to the right of the cash register. Besides the store phone, my cell phone is on there, as well. Oh, and Angus is in his bed behind the counter. He had a big morning and will probably nap all afternoon."

"Very well," Mrs. Patrick said. "I'm sure Angus — whatever that is — will be fine. And I'll call your cell should I need anything else."

We walked outside. Vera and I exchanged good-byes, but Riley seemed eager to get to MacKenzies' Mochas. I wasn't eager to get there at all. I had an idea that my visit to her father had prompted this meeting, and although Riley seemed to be playing nice at the moment, I wasn't naive enough to believe she'd suddenly decided to be my best friend.

I opened the heavy wooden door to MacKenzies' Mochas and allowed Riley to precede me inside. I took a second to breathe in the coffee-laden aromas.

The shop had been a bar before Sadie and Blake renovated it. They kept the long, polished bar down the middle of the floor, and placed wooden tables and chairs throughout the rest of the shop. On shelves behind the bar, there were McKenzies'

Mochas mugs for sale (logo mugs and plain mugs that were replicas of the cup in the logo). I had a set of each.

The shelves also contained house-blend coffees for sale, chocolate-covered coffee and espresso beans, biscotti, and other packaged goods. Covered cake plates situated along the bar displayed the day's muffins, pies, and other pastries. The counter behind the bar was where the coffeemakers, cappuccino machines, and espresso machines were located.

Sadie's eyes nearly bugged out of her head when she saw me walk in with Riley. She reminded me of Ricky Ricardo, and I imagined I'd have some 'splainin' to do.

Sadie handed us menus and asked what we'd like to drink. I opted for a diet soda, and Riley ordered a latte with a glass of ice water on the side. Sadie invited us to take a seat and said she'd bring our drinks over.

Riley chose a table in the back corner. "Is this all right?"

I nodded and took my seat.

"I thought it would afford us some privacy so we can chat," she said.

"Great. What would you like to chat about?"

"I think you know."

She was mistaken if she thought I was tak-

160

ing the initial plunge off *that* particular diving board. Rather, I remained silent, smiled slightly, and gazed around the café as if I had never seen the decor before. Antique skis and ski equipment adorned the walls, along with pictures of people who appeared to have been living in the 1920s and enjoying skiing and various other outdoor sports.

"I understand you paid a visit to my father yesterday."

I met Riley's straightforward stare. "I did. He's charming."

"He can be when it suits him."

Sadie brought our drinks, and then asked if we were ready to order. Riley and I both ordered the chicken salad on croissants with a side of sea-salt chips.

Sadie departed, and Riley sipped her latte, gazing at me over the rim of her cup.

She lowered the cup. "Dad was impressed with you. He said you were gutsy." She inclined her head. "It did take guts for you to go visit Dad. Why did you?"

"He seemed like one of the last resources to provide me with some answers. I'm very upset that two men have visited the storeroom in my shop and were later found dead, and I'm really worried that the police apparently think my friend or I might have something to do with it. I've lived in Tallulah Falls for less than two months, Riley, and I'm beginning to wonder if I made a mistake in coming here."

Sadie returned with our croissants and left reluctantly, after we assured her we needed nothing else.

"So what did Dad tell you?" Riley asked.

"He basically told me to be careful. What did he tell you?"

"He basically told me to help you. I think the possibility that Bill Trelawney was killed by the fifth member of Four Square — the one only he knew about — has Dad on edge."

Once I was back at work, I phoned Todd at the Brew Crew.

"Hi, Marcy. Are you still planning on stopping by after work?"

"I am, but I may be a few minutes later than I'd anticipated. I'm expecting Sadie to be here to ask a thousand and one questions later this afternoon."

"Why? What's up?"

"When Riley called this morning and invited me to lunch, I figured it had something to do with my visit to her father."

"Did it?"

"Oh yes. That's why I rushed you out of the shop this morning. I didn't want Vera to know we'd visited Norman Patrick."

"No, I can't blame you there. Vera means well, but she can be Tallulah Falls' one-stop news outlet."

"I'm glad you understand. I was so afraid that either you or I would give away too much information, and Vera would figure it out. I suppose it's not that big a deal if Vera knew, but . . ."

"You don't want *everyone* knowing."

"Exactly. As a matter of fact, I'd have preferred Riley not knowing. Of course, Mr. Patrick is her dad, so I really shouldn't have been surprised that he called and told her about our visit. But when she phoned me this morning, I half expected her to slap me with a restraining order or something."

"Nah. I think she's pretty tough, but Riley's fair."

"Oh. Do you know her well, then?"

"I suppose. I've known her for years."

Detective Nash walked into the shop. He was dressed in a dark suit with a light blue tie, and I thought the blue brought out his eyes. Then I wondered why I was thinking about his eyes.

"I'm sorry, but I have to go," I said. "I'll talk with you later this evening."

"I'll be looking forward to it."

I turned the phone off and smiled at

Detective Nash. "Good afternoon, sir. May I interest you in some yarn?"

He grinned. "Depends. What kind of yarn are you going to tell me?"

I bit my lower lip. "What kind do you want to hear?"

With a crook of his index finger, he beckoned me to leave the counter and join him in the sitting area. We sat on the navy sofa that was facing away from the door.

"I'd like you to tell me the story in which common sense prevailed and you changed your mind about going to the prison yesterday," Detective Nash said. "But since I know that didn't happen, why don't you tell me how your interrogation went?"

"Mr. Patrick admitted he'd worked with Timothy Enright, though not through Four Square Development. He said he'd done legal work for Mr. Enright."

"Makes sense. Norm Patrick did legal work for most of the town."

"He also told me Timothy didn't go bankrupt like Lorraine led me to believe."

"Anything else?"

"Riley Kendall bought me lunch today."

Detective Nash raised his brows.

"It seems her dad called and . . . he . . . um . . . asked her to help me out."

He chuckled. "You have quite a way with

164

people, you know that? Either you beguile them to the point where they'd do anything to protect you, or you frustrate them to the point where they want to kill you."

"So which way do you feel about me?"

He looked at me for a long moment, seemingly not willing to answer. I realized that my heart was pounding in my chest.

He jumped up like he suddenly remembered he needed to be somewhere, told me Chief Myers would fire him if he knew he was visiting me, and left.

That afternoon I sat in my favorite red chair with Angus softly snoring at my feet. Luckily, no customers had come by during the lunch hour when Camille was watching the shop. But after lunch business had picked up and Sarah Crenshaw had come in, followed by a carful of cheery Chicagoan tourists who told me they were on an "antiquing-adventure road trip." They also happened to be enthusiastic needlecrafters and were very pleasantly complimentary about the Seven-Year Stitch. They had gushed over everything — the layout, the selection, the cozy chairs, even the shaggy shop mascot, Mr. O'Ruff. I was blushing by the time they were done, and also happy that they'd each walked away with a few kits and had decimated my basket of perle flosses. I'd had to run to the storeroom to restock. Fortunately, the perle flosses weren't near where Mr. Enright had been found, but the storeroom still gave me the creeps. I was sure the feeling would subside in time, but for the moment . . .

Now the afternoon was almost gone, but Sadie hadn't been over yet. I found that a bit odd. I found a lot of things odd these days. Mostly, though, I kept going over my lunch conversation with Riley. She had said her father had called last night and asked if she'd met me.

"I've met her," Riley had said.

According to her, their phone call had progressed like this.

"You don't seem to like her much," Mr. Patrick had said.

"I barely know her. I've only met her once."

"Well, maybe you should get to know Tinkerbell, Ri. I think she's probably a good kid."

He'd gone on to tell her about our visit and had finished with, "Sounds like she could use a few more friends, what with people in Tallulah Falls dropping like flies off a bug zapper."

Riley implied he'd wanted her to be one

of my new friends. But I was skeptical. Maybe he'd merely called and asked Riley to keep an eye on me . . . to find out what, if anything, I was learning about Four Square Development. Or maybe to set me up.

I wanted to learn more about the other men involved in the Four Square Development scandal. I needed to know the identity of Bill Trelawney's crony. Surely someone else knew.

Chapter Nine

When I got home, I took Angus inside and we went straight upstairs to the bedroom. My plan was to get into my pajamas, prop up in bed, and watch TV for a while. There was a message on my answering machine. I expected it to be either Sadie or Mom. I was wrong. It was Margaret Trelawney. She must have gotten my landline number from my lease.

"Marcy," she said. "Can you help me? I think somebody is trying to kill me."

The message had been left more than an hour ago. I couldn't really imagine why Mrs. Trelawney would call *me* instead of the police if she really thought she was in danger, but I dialed her number, and Sylvia answered.

"Hi, Sylvia," I said. "I'm really sorry to disturb you, but may I please speak with Mrs. Trelawney?"

"I'm sorry, but Maggie has already gone

to bed."

"I see. Well, she left a message on my answering machine earlier this evening. Normally, I wouldn't have returned her call this late, but she sounded upset."

"She did have . . . an episode earlier. She was so distraught, I gave her one of the sedatives her doctor prescribed."

"I'm sorry," I said. "I can't even imagine what she must be going through. In the morning, please let her know I returned her call and tell her I'll try to stop by."

"Very well," Sylvia said. "Goodnight, Ms. Singer."

I hung up, and almost immediately the phone rang. I picked up the receiver.

"Marcy," Mrs. Trelawney whispered. "It's me."

"Oh, hello, Mrs. Trelawney. I hope I didn't wake you when I phoned."

"No. I was awake. I didn't take that pill Sylvia gave me. I need my wits about me."

She'd seemed frantic when she'd left the message. Now she sounded strangely calm.

"I think whoever killed Bill wants me dead, too," she continued. "Chief Myers says it's all a big mistake and that Bill's death was the result of a robbery gone wrong. You told me you believe he and Mr. Enright were killed by the same people. I

169

think so, too."

So that explained it. Mrs. Trelawney saw me as the only person who was convinced this was a larger conspiracy.

"What did Chief Myers say about that?"

"He and Sylvia whispered around, and I think he encouraged her to keep me sedated. But, as I already told you, I'm keeping my wits about me."

"Mrs. Trelawney, what makes you think you're in danger?"

"Because it makes sense. Timothy Enright knew too much, Bill knew too much, and I know too much."

"Too much about what?"

"About that whole Four Square Development mess."

I could hardly believe she was actually admitting her husband was involved with Four Square Development.

"Timothy must've known about it, too," she continued. "Bill told me what he'd scratched on the wall. It scared him."

"It scared Mr. Trelawney? Why?"

"Because he was afraid that if Timothy had told anyone else the identity of Four Square Development's silent partner, we would all be killed." She sniffled. "He was right, wasn't he?"

"Who was the partner?" I asked. "If you

believe he killed Timothy and your husband, we'll call Chief Myers or Ted Nash as soon as we hang up and have the guy picked up. Then he won't be a threat to you anymore."

"That's just it, dear. I don't know who he was."

"You mean, Mr. Trelawney didn't tell you?"

"He was afraid to. He said the less I knew about Four Square Development, the better."

"But, then, how can you think you know too much?"

"Because I do, dear. I know this person is the killer. And I know he'll come after me, too."

"I won't let anything happen to you, Mrs. Trelawney," I said.

But it was a promise I was afraid I'd be unable to keep. I knew it, and so did Mrs. Trelawney.

I ran by MacKenzies' Mochas for a latte before opening the shop the next morning. Blake was at the counter.

"You're in early," he said.

"Yeah, I woke up early and didn't see any use to just sitting around the house." I looked around the café. "Where's Sadie?"

"Home. She got sick yesterday afternoon.

I think it's probably a stomach bug, but if she doesn't feel better by midmorning, she's going to call the doctor."

"I'm sorry she's feeling so lousy," I said. "I can cancel classes this evening and work for you so you can go home and take care of her, if you want me to."

"I appreciate that," Blake said, "but my evening manager is coming in after the lunch rush so I can get on out of here."

"Oh, that's good."

"Low-fat vanilla with a hint of cinnamon, right?"

I nodded, and he deftly prepared my latte.

He turned back to me with a grin. "At first, I thought Sadie was simply sick from not knowing what you were doing in here with Riley Kendall. But then it became apparent to both of us that she really was physically ill."

Blake handed me the latte, and I inhaled, the soft vanilla and woody cinnamon blending beautifully with the underlying rich coffee. "Tell her I hope she's feeling better," I said as I paid for my drink, "and that I'll fill you both in on what little there is to tell about Riley as soon as she's up to it."

"Will do, Marcy."

I went to the shop and unlocked the door. Angus barreled through ahead of me. The scroll frames I'd ordered had arrived on Saturday, and I needed to make room to display a few of them before customers began to arrive. I was able to combine two short rows of wooden hoops into one long row and place the scroll frames on the newly vacant row.

I was standing back a short distance with my hands on my hips, surveying the display, when the door opened.

"You look proud of yourself," Ted Nash said as Angus trotted over to greet him.

Ted was dropping by a lot lately, and I was beginning to think the case was just an excuse. Maybe Vera was right and he *had* "set his cap" for me. A vision of Todd flitted through my mind at that thought, but I told myself to keep any thoughts of romance reined in until the Enright and Trelawney cases had been resolved.

"I am proud of myself," I said. "Don't you think this looks nice?"

He grinned. "I think it looks great." He scratched Angus' head.

"So, he doesn't make you nervous anymore?"

"Nope. I guess we've become accustomed to each other." He cocked his head toward the display. "It was those frame things that prompted you to come in to work early?"

"Not exactly. I just happened to be in the neighborhood a little earlier than usual. You?"

"I just happened to be in the neighborhood myself," he said. "When I saw you were here, I decided to say hello."

"I'm glad you did. Do you feel there's any reason that whoever killed Mr. Trelawney would now be gunning for his wife?"

Detective Nash rocked back on his heels and shoved his hands into his pockets. "Why do you ask?"

"Why do you ask why I ask instead of answering the question?"

He tucked his chin and began walking toward the sitting area. "I asked Chief Myers to put officers on patrol at the Trelawney house the instant I learned Bill had been shot. That was partially with the expectation that the shooter might go to the home, looking for something." He turned back toward me. "But it was also to protect Mrs. Trelawney. It stands to reason that if robbery wasn't a factor in Bill's death, then the shooter might have a grudge against both the husband and his wife. Now tell me what you know."

I moved over to stand in front of him. "She's scared, Ted . . . I mean, Detective Nash."

"Ted is fine," he said.

Trying to pretend I hadn't made that faux pas, I went back to explaining about Mrs. Trelawney. "She called me yesterday and left a message on my answering machine. By the time I was able to call her back, Sylvia answered and said Mrs. Trelawney had gone to bed. But then Mrs. Trelawney called me right back."

"Had Sylvia told her to call?"

"Oh, no. In fact, Mrs. Trelawney was rather secretive about her call."

"What did she say?" he asked.

"She's convinced the same person who killed her husband is going to kill her, too."

"Did she say what led her to believe this?"

"She says she knows too much about Four Square Development. She says she doesn't know who Bill was working with there, but she thinks that person killed both him and Timothy Enright."

Angus brought his tennis ball over and dropped it at Ted's feet. The detective picked up the ball and rolled it across the floor. Angus bounded after it.

"Will you be at Bill Trelawney's service this evening?" Detective Nash asked.

"I'll be at the visitation," I said, "but I need to get back here before the funeral. I have a class."

"I'll be at the funeral. If Margaret Trelawney gives you any information, whether you think it's important or not" — he handed me his business card — "call my cell phone and let me know."

I handed back the card. "I've already got one of these. You gave it to me the day I found . . . you know, the day we met."

His mouth turned down at the corners. "Huh. I figured you might've thrown it away." He handed back the card. "Keep it. That way you'll always have one handy."

"Do you think someone really is after Mrs. Trelawney?" I asked.

Detective Nash sighed and rubbed the back of his neck. "I'm afraid it's a strong possibility. I think you and I both believe that Tim Enright and Bill Trelawney were killed because of something they knew. And if a husband knows something, odds are his wife does, too."

"Not necessarily," I said.

"True." He inclined his head. "But if you'd already killed two people to keep your secret safe, would you risk the chance of a third person knowing?"

"One other thing," I said. "Chief Myers told Mrs. Trelawney that Bill's murder was definitely a robbery, but you said *if.* Does the department think now it was, in fact, a robbery gone wrong?"

Ted frowned. "Did Mrs. Trelawney tell you that's what Chief Myers said?"

I nodded.

"Then he must've told her that to try to ease her mind. When Bill Trelawney was found, his wallet contained more than three hundred dollars that hadn't been touched."

CHAPTER TEN

I went by the house to bathe, change clothes, and drop off Angus before going to Bill Trelawney's visitation. I wore a navy pencil skirt, a white button-down blouse, and a triple strand of pearls. My intention was to greet Mrs. Trelawney, once again express my sympathy, and then make a discreet exit before the funeral started.

I had barely known him . . . or his wife, for that matter. But Mr. Trelawney had always been pleasant to me. He'd loved to chat, so I could — up until now — anticipate collection of the rent to be a drawn-out, time-consuming affair. Blake liked to joke that it took Mr. Trelawney a month to collect the rent from all of his lessees because he made it a daily undertaking so he could tell the same stories to different people. For me, the conversations with Mr. Trelawney had always been amiable and interesting.

For some reason, that thought brought to mind Ted Nash's grim question: *If you'd already killed two people to keep your secret safe, would you risk the chance of a third person knowing?*

It was a safe bet that anything the talkative Bill Trelawney knew, his wife knew also.

I pulled into the parking lot, glad it didn't appear to be overly crowded yet. Keeping my skirt in place, I slid carefully out of the Jeep. A hand took hold of my elbow to steady me as I made my descent. I turned, pleasantly surprised to see Todd.

"Thank you," I told him.

"Anytime," he said. "It must be a lot trickier to get in and out of that Jeep in a skirt than it is when you're wearing jeans."

"A *lot* trickier. Are you staying for the funeral?"

"No. I just want to pay my respects to the family."

"Me, too," I said. "I have a class tonight, and I need to be there even if none of my students show up."

"It'll likely be a slow night at the Brew Crew, too."

"Mind if I stop by after class?"

He smiled. "I'd be disappointed if you didn't."

We went on into the funeral home and

stood in line to speak with Mrs. Trelawney. I recognized Riley Kendall several people ahead of us. She was with a tall, dark-skinned man whom I recognized from the photographs in her office. It was also evident he was her husband from the way his hand lingered proprietarily at the small of her back.

The door opened, chilling me with a blast of cool air. I glanced over my shoulder and saw Vera Langhorne coming in.

"Hello, Marcy," she said, hurrying over to me. "I want you to meet my husband, John." She looked up at her husband, who was not only tall but painfully thin. "John, this is Marcy Singer."

Mr. Langhorne extended his hand. It felt cold and brittle, and I ended the handshake as quickly as possible without appearing rude.

"Ms. Singer," he said, "I've heard great things about you. To hear Vera extol your talents, one would think you are the Picasso of needlecraft."

I laughed softly. "Vera is too kind. She's becoming quite the cross-stitch artist herself."

"Indeed." He smiled at his wife. "I'm proud of her." He nodded at Todd. "Calloway, how are you this evening?"

"I'm fine, sir. Thank you. You?"

While the men engaged in small talk, Vera pulled me to the side.

"I'd planned on seeing Margaret and then coming on to class," she said. "But John asked me to stay."

"Of course. I understand."

"He has to return to the bank to fax some papers that were due today or something." She fluttered a hand dismissively. "But I'll be in tomorrow morning for a sit-'n'-stitch."

"Fantastic. I'll look forward to seeing you then."

Another couple approached the Langhornes and engaged them in conversation, so Todd and I made small talk as we inched along in the line. Finally, we came to Sylvia and Mrs. Trelawney. Sylvia was standing, as if to underscore the fact that she was the stronger of the two. Mrs. Trelawney was sitting on a padded folding chair at the head of her husband's closed casket.

I nodded and spoke to Sylvia, then averted my eyes from the casket as I approached Mrs. Trelawney.

"How are you?" I asked softly, stooping down and taking her hand.

She smiled. "Oh, I'm fine, dear. And don't you look beautiful? That beau of yours is a lucky fellow."

"Thank you." I straightened. "If you need anything —"

"I'll sure let you know, dear," she said. "You're ever so kind."

I glanced back at Sylvia, who shot me a triumphant smirk. One way or another, she'd gotten Mrs. Trelawney to take a sedative . . . or two.

When we got out to the parking lot, Todd walked me to the Jeep. "Do you think poor Mrs. Trelawney even knows what's going on tonight?"

"I don't think she has the faintest idea," I said. "And I'm not certain that's a good thing." I was thinking that if someone did intend to harm her, she shouldn't be all doped up.

"No, I'm not, either," Todd said. "She needs some closure, and she isn't going to get it like that."

"She was terribly distraught last night. So maybe . . ." I shrugged.

Todd kissed my cheek and said he'd talk with me later.

The clock on my dashboard let me know I didn't have time to go home and change clothes before class, so I hurried on to the shop. By the time I got there, Julie and Amber were sitting in their car, waiting for me.

"Sorry I'm late," I said as we exited our vehicles and I unlocked the shop. "I went by to pay my condolences to Mrs. Trelawney."

"We didn't know Mr. Trelawney," Julie said. "He was your landlord?"

"That's right. I believe the Trelawneys own the shops on both sides of this street."

"Wow," Julie said, following me inside the shop. "Must be nice." She looked as if she had a sudden inspiration. "Oh, Amber, would you run back to the car and get your school photos for Marcy to see?" She handed her car keys to her daughter.

"Oh, Mom," Amber groaned. "Marcy doesn't want to see those."

"No, I'd love to see them," I said.

"See?" Julie asked.

With a dramatic eye roll, Amber went back outside to get the photos.

Julie spoke quietly and quickly. "You need to have your credit report run if you haven't done so since moving here."

"But why? I —"

"You may be the victim of identity theft. Here comes Amber. I'll explain it in a minute."

Amber opened the door and held the envelope out to me as if it were contaminated. "They're not any good. I look like a dork."

I took the eight-by-tens out of the envelope and drew in a breath. "Amber, these are gorgeous!" They really were.

"No, they're not." She tried to appear unaffected, but I could tell she was really pleased by the praise.

"May I have one?" I asked. "If there are any left after all the relatives, I mean."

"By all means," Julie said.

I slid the photos back into the envelope and handed it to Julie. Julie, in turn, handed the envelope to Amber and asked her to return it to the car.

Once Amber was out of earshot, Julie explained why I needed to have a credit report run. "I work for a collections agency, and yesterday a delinquent credit card account came across my desk with the name Marcy Singer. I called the home number, and a man answered. He said you were at work at the hospital."

"Do you think it could be another Marcy Singer?" I asked.

"Maybe. But since that Four Square mess last year, we've seen more stolen identities than you can imagine. You should look into it, just to be safe."

"Thank you. I will."

"Just don't mention it around Amber. Her dad was a straw buyer for Four Square. He got only probation and a fine, but we're trying to put the whole nightmare behind us."

"Why do you guys look so serious?" Amber asked as she opened the door.

"Because you're seriously beautiful," I said, "and we're thinking up ways to scare the boys off." I looked at Julie. "Yes, you can borrow Angus anytime."

We were rewarded with another eye roll before we migrated to the sitting area to start class.

Amber had come a lot further along in her design than her mother had. Her mother pointed out that Amber had more free time, but Amber protested, "At least you don't have homework, Mom!"

Amber's design was a monarch butterfly on a yellow rose. Her tote bag was natural canvas, and the background was sky blue.

"You know, Amber," I said, "I was a little concerned about your choosing this design because it involves such intricate work for a beginner. But this looks great. You're doing a wonderful job."

"Thanks, Marcy." She looked up at me with a huge grin.

Julie was doing a snowman. It was simple but cute. She had started from the top and, so far, had the hat almost completed.

Although it was just the three of us — or maybe because it was just the three of us — we had a pleasant, relaxing class. I was even able to forget about Julie's warning about identity theft until class was over.

After class, I went over and had a soda at the Brew Crew. I chatted briefly with Todd, but he was busier than expected and didn't have much time to socialize.

I was glad to get home and into my flannel pj's with the bunnies on them. I wasn't used to sitting around in dress clothes all evening. So now I was sitting by the fire with Angus on one side and my rolling embroidery kit on the other. I had called my credit card company and they didn't report any unusual activity, so then I had left a message for Mom's attorney to dig deeper and assure me I was not a victim of identity theft. Somehow, despite all the trouble surrounding the shop, my life seemed pretty sweet.

My embroidery kit has three drawers — two large and one small — and holds my works in progress, patterns, threads, needles, hoops, scissors, and frames. My plan was to spend the rest of the evening working on the replica of the MacKenzies' Mochas logo

I was making Blake and Sadie for Christmas.

As I stitched, I thought about Julie saying her husband had been a straw buyer for Four Square. Why would a man with such a lovely wife and daughter subject himself to the possibility of going to prison? I figured money was the reason, naturally; but now that he was on probation, for restitution, he probably had to pay back more than he initially earned, and his daughter was ashamed of him. Tears pricked the backs of my eyes. Poor Amber.

The phone rang. It was Alfred Benton, Mom's attorney.

"Alfred, you didn't have to call me back tonight," I said.

"I know, but I wanted to make sure you hadn't found another body in your storeroom."

"Not this time." I explained about Julie's concern that my identity had been compromised.

Alfred assured me he'd look into the matter first thing the next morning. "I'm assuming I'm to keep mum to your mum?"

"For now, please. After all, it might just be a misunderstanding."

You have no idea how indebted I am to this man. He's been my mother's lawyer for nearly thirty years and my secret keeper for almost that long. He was often the closest thing I had to a father.

Angus groaned in his sleep, and his foot twitched. It was an inconsequential movement, but it nudged me back to the present. I went back to work on the MacKenzies' Mochas logo, and sometime later, like Angus, drifted off to sleep.

CHAPTER ELEVEN

I felt as if I had cobwebs in my eyes when I stepped into MacKenzies' Mochas the next morning.

Blake gave me an exaggerated blink. "You look like something Angus chewed up and spit out. You don't have this stomach virus, too, do you?"

"No." I lowered myself onto a stool and propped my head on my hand. "I just didn't sleep well last night."

Blake shook his head and made me a latte. "That's getting to be a habit with you."

"I know. Did Sadie go to the doctor yesterday?" I asked.

"Yep. She had a stomach virus."

"I'm glad it was nothing serious."

"Me, too." He sat the latte on a paper coaster in front of me. "It wasn't what she was hoping for, though."

I tilted my head.

"She hoped she was pregnant," Blake said.

"Oh, Blake! Sadie didn't even tell me you guys are trying to have a baby."

"Why do you think she was so fired up about your moving to Tallulah Falls? We're eventually going to need a reliable baby-sitter." He smiled. "I'm kidding. When you talk to Sadie, though, don't let her know I told you we're working on a baby. She doesn't want anyone to know until it's a done deal."

I promised not to tell and said I would call to check on Sadie later in the day.

"By the way," Blake said, "there were some people in earlier this morning saying someone broke into the Trelawney house during the funeral last night."

"That's horrible! Did they catch whoever did it?"

"No, I don't think so."

"Do the police think whoever it was is the person who killed Bill?"

Blake shrugged. "I don't know. Just repeating idle gossip. I feel really bad for Mrs. Trelawney, though."

"Me, too. That must've scared her half to death."

"Well, thank goodness the break-in happened while no one was at home."

I finished my latte and hurried next door to work.

I hadn't been there long when Reggie paid me a visit. She was wearing an ankle-length, floral-print dress and a pink pashmina. She looked lovely, and I told her so.

She smiled. "Thank you. You look like a woman who has too much on her mind."

I nodded. "The list grows longer every day. Do you think I should simply pack everything up and return to San Francisco?"

"Only you can answer that question," Reggie said. "Do you honestly feel that coming here to Tallulah Falls was a mistake? Or are you upset over what happened to Margaret Trelawney last night?"

"I don't know. I just heard about the break-in from Blake MacKenzie. I'm upset for Mrs. Trelawney, of course, but her current predicament is only the latest log on the fire." I sighed.

Reggie looked pointedly at her watch. "The Seven-Year Stitch doesn't officially open this morning for another ninety minutes. I thought you and I could jaunt over to the Trelawneys' home and check on Margaret."

"That's a flimsy ruse for snooping around their house, isn't it?"

"Not at all." She dangled her car keys. "Come on. I'm driving."

Reggie's immaculate Subaru was easier to

get in and out of than my Jeep, but I still preferred my big Jeep. It suited me somehow. I also preferred doing the driving. Reggie's driving was fine — she obeyed all speed limits and traffic rules, as a proper police officer's wife should — but I like to be in the driver's seat. It's difficult for me to relinquish control . . . of anything.

"So, what are we looking for?" I asked, as Reggie parked in the Trelawneys' driveway.

"The same thing the burglar was looking for."

"Which is?"

Reggie scowled slightly. "I'll know it when I see it."

I shook my head. "How do you think we're going to find anything relevant that was overlooked by not only the burglar but also by police crime-scene investigators?"

"I don't know, but it's worth a shot." She looked at me. "Isn't it?"

Before I could answer, Sylvia flung open the front door. "Who are you? What are you doing here?"

Reggie and I stepped out of the car.

"It's Reggie Singh, Sylvia. Marcy Singer is with me. We've come to see Margaret."

"Okay. Come in, then."

Sylvia looked as rough that morning as I felt. Although she wore a beautiful beige suit with a chocolate brown silk shirt and matching shoes, her eyes reflected the strain and lack of sleep the past several hours had wrought.

"How are you holding up?" I asked her.

"I want to go home," she said. "I want to go home until Bill's murderer has been apprehended. In fact, I am going home. And I want to take Maggie with me."

"Did something happen last night after Chief Myers left?" Reggie asked.

Sylvia shook her head. "It was unsettling being here. That's all."

"I'm sure it was. Why don't you gather up some things for yourself and for Margaret, and Marcy and I will wait and see you out."

"I'm already packed," she said, "but I'll pack a suitcase for Maggie. She's in the den, by the way." Sylvia left the living room and walked down the hall.

Reggie and I went into the den. Mrs. Trelawney was sweeping up some of the debris scattered about the room.

"Mrs. Trelawney, I can do that," I said.

She relinquished the broom and dustpan readily enough and sank onto the sofa. "Bill used this room for his office." She closed her eyes and shook her head. "What a mess."

"Maggie, do you mind if I take a look

around? See if there's . . . well, I don't really know what I'm looking for."

Mrs. Trelawney gave Reggie a defeated wave. "Fine, fine. Whatever you like."

Reggie sat down at the desk and began opening drawers, while I sat with Mrs. Trelawney on the couch. In a few minutes, she said, "Marcy, come take a look at this."

I went to the desk to see that she was poring over an accounting ledger. It gave me a somewhat unwelcome flashback to all those years of doing payroll and bookkeeping. This particular ledger appeared to be accounts receivable for Mr. Trelawney's rental clients.

Reggie turned and looked up at me, her face expectant. "Do you see it?"

"I'm afraid not."

"Look closer." She ran her finger down the lined page. "By some of these names you can see a small notation: *b*."

"You think these people were behind on their accounts?"

"No. I think it means they were straw buyers."

I frowned. "That's quite a leap, isn't it? What makes you think the *b* stands for straw buyers?"

"This ledger is dated 2004. Notice there are squares around each of the letters? I

194

think this is a dummy ledger with coded information for Four Square Development. That would explain why such an old ledger is being used."

"Once again, Reggie, that's a stretch. Just because there are blocks around the year, you think it's synonymous with Four Square?"

"Maybe it is a stretch," she said, "but right now it's all we have. None of the other ledgers have squares around the years. So yes, I think this ledger has information relevant to Four Square. I believe the intruder was looking for something but had no idea what," Reggie said.

"Give it to your husband, won't you?" Mrs. Trelawney asked. "Ask him to make sure Chief Myers gets it."

I was once again sitting in my favorite red chair in the shop's seating area, working on my tote bag. Angus was snoring softly at my feet, and I was having trouble not dozing off myself. It was terribly rainy today. A few people had drifted in and out, buying yarn, cross-stitch fabric, and thread, but overall business had been slow.

All day I'd been planning my evening. As soon as I got home, I'd take a warm, relaxing bath. Then I'd have a bowl of clam chowder. And then Angus and I would turn in early, maybe watch a little mindless television before actually calling it a night.

I yawned and stretched. It was still nearly an hour until closing time, so I decided to call Sadie. That would wake me up and, hopefully, it would be a good time for her to talk.

She answered on the third ring.

"Is this a bad time?" I asked.

"No. I was just lying on the sofa, and the phone was on the other side of the room."

"I'm sorry."

"Don't apologize. I should've had the phone with me. How've you been these past couple days?"

"Me?" I asked. "It's you I'm worried about."

"Ah, I'll do. I'm getting over the bug. I probably needed to lose a few pounds, anyway."

"If I didn't have so much other junk going on, I might be tempted to come have you breathe on me. It would be cheaper than liposuction."

"As if you need to lose an ounce," she said. "Blake told me someone broke into the Trelawney house during Bill's funeral."

"Yeah. It was terrible. Mrs. Trelawney has gone to stay with Sylvia in Portland for a

196

few days."

"Sylvia the dragon lady? Poor Mrs. Trelawney. She must be scared."

"She is. And Sylvia is, too. I think at first Sylvia thought Mrs. Trelawney was being foolish and paranoid, but she's had a change of heart."

"Because of the break-in," Sadie asked, "or did something else happen?"

"I'm not sure. When Reggie and I stopped by this morning to see about Mrs. Trelawney, Sylvia was already packed and ready to leave."

"That's odd."

"I am glad Mrs. Trelawney decided to stay with Sylvia for a few days," I said. "I feel it's best that she get out of town for the time being."

"Not to change the subject," Sadie said, effectively changing the subject, "but have you heard from Todd lately?"

"I saw him at Mr. Trelawney's visitation. We like each other, Sadie, but our schedules aren't that compatible right now."

"It'll work out. Things always work out."

Her voice sounded wistful as she said that, and I somehow felt she was no longer talking about Todd and me but about her own disappointment over not being pregnant.

"It will," I said. "Everything will work out great."

I decided not to burden Sadie with any further talk of my currently troubled life.

After speaking with her, I saw there were still a few minutes left until closing time. Angus was still snoring, and the sound seemed somehow hypnotic. I allowed my head to loll against the back of the chair and my heavy eyelids to close.

Only for a second . . . So tired . . .

I was surrounded. Most of the people I knew from Tallulah Falls were there. Sadie, Blake, Todd, Riley, Mrs. Patrick . . . even Timothy Enright, his estranged wife (or should I say, his *strange* wife), and Bill Trelawney were there. For some reason, they all began throwing straw at me.

I was jolted by a loud, musical trill. It still took me a second to shake off the dream and answer my phone.

It was Alfred Benton. "Marcella, darling," he said, "I'm sorry to tell you that your financial identity has indeed been compromised."

CHAPTER TWELVE

That certainly woke me up. I bolted upright in my chair, making Angus get up and move over to his bed behind the counter.

"What exactly does this mean, Alfred?"

His response was slow and deliberate. "I don't know the full extent to which your credit was used at this time. However, you should cancel all your credit cards, flag your other financial accounts for possible fraud activity, and alert the authorities."

I had half a dozen questions, and they began pouring out all at once. "Who could've done this? What about my checking account? Can I use that? How did this happen? You haven't told my mom, have you?"

"One thing at a time, sweetheart," Alfred said. "I have not told your mother anything. Your checking account is fine, although you need to have your bank be watchful for any suspicious activity. And the issuing financial institutions should be able to replace your credit cards within a week to ten days."

I sighed.

"In the meantime, if you need to put something on a credit card, I can give you the number for one of mine."

"Oh, no, Alfred. I'm sure I can live without a credit card for a week. How much trouble am I in?"

"It's nothing I can't get you out of."

"Why don't I find that reassuring?" I asked.

He chuckled. "My paralegals will have a bit more work and perhaps get to delve into new legal territory, that's all."

"New legal territory such as?"

"Real estate fraud," he answered. "It appears someone posing as you bought a piece of real estate in northern Oregon and then sold it for a small fortune. I knew that couldn't be you, and I flagged it."

"You . . . you mean this person — whoever conducted this transaction — was a straw buyer?"

"Yes, I imagine so. Hmmm. I'm surprised you're familiar with that term, Marcella, darling."

My stomach sank. "I . . . uh . . . I just learned about it recently."

"Well, not to worry. I'll take care of all of

this. I or my staff will call you if there's anything we need from you. All right?"

"Alfred, is there any indication who might've done this to me?"

"None yet, but if something turns up, I'll let you know."

I caught up with Reggie in the library parking lot. She was almost to her car when I drove up slowly beside her.

She turned, and I put down my window.

"Hi, Marcy. What's going on? Do you need something from the library?"

"No, but I'd like to talk with you. Is Manu working this evening? I thought maybe you could join me for dinner."

"Manu isn't working this evening, but I can call and see if he has plans." She paused. "Or is this girl talk?"

"It's stolen-identity talk."

She raised her brows. "As in *your identity* or someone else's?"

"Mine."

"Where would you like us to meet you for dinner?"

"Would you guys mind coming to my house?" I asked. "I don't want to leave Angus alone for another evening. Plus, I was already planning on making clam chowder and cheese biscuits."

201

"Is six thirty okay?"

"Six thirty is great."

So, I wouldn't be having my turning-in-early evening, after all. Of course, that was a given the instant Alfred told me my identity had been stolen. I desperately needed to talk this situation through with someone, and I didn't want to go to Chief Myers. After what I'd heard, I found the man a little intimidating and didn't think I'd find a sympathetic ear, so I hoped Manu and Reggie could steer me in the right direction.

Manu and Reggie arrived at about quarter past six with a bottle of white wine.

"Thanks," I said, "but you didn't need to bring a thing except your steel-trap minds."

Manu held up the bottle. "Then perhaps we should save this for another time," he said with a smile.

His wife playfully backhanded his arm. "You're silly. When have you ever known either of us to overindulge?"

"I'd never known Timothy Enright to overindulge, but you saw him yourself the night of Marcy's open house."

Reggie shook her head. "I saw it, but I still don't understand it."

"But I thought the police suspected Mr.

Enright of having been poisoned," I said.

"We do," Manu said. "But that doesn't mean he wasn't drunk at your party."

"Do you suppose there's a drug that could make someone feel and behave as if they were drunk?" I asked.

"Oh, sure." Manu shrugged. "Lots of pain meds make people act loopy."

"So Mr. Enright could have received an overdose of some sort of pain medication, right?" I asked.

"It's possible," Manu said, "but he hadn't been prescribed any pain medications, and he hadn't suffered any recent accidents. We'll know more, though, when we get the autopsy report."

Reggie took the ledger from the recesses of her roomy tote. "I didn't get a chance to look at this during work today. I thought we could go over it either before or after dinner."

Manu's eyes narrowed. "Rajani Singh, where did you get that ledger?"

Reggie blinked. "Mrs. Trelawney asked me to give it to you to pass on to Chief Myers. I had to get to work, so this is the first opportunity I've had."

I took the bottle of wine from him. "Dinner is almost ready. Let's go on into the kitchen."

I took the cheese biscuits out of the oven and placed them in a bread basket. Fortunately, Angus was in the backyard for the time being. He loves cheese biscuits.

As I poured the clam chowder into a soup tureen, Manu and Reggie sat down at the table. I placed both the tureen and the bread basket on the table. I handed Manu a corkscrew and asked if he would do the honors while I retrieved three of the crystal wineglasses Mom had sent me as a house-warming gift.

Manu popped the cork and filled our glasses. He then raised his for a toast. "To the brighter day we know is coming."

We gently clinked our glasses.

"Do you really believe that, Manu?" I asked.

"Of course," he said, ladling chowder into his bowl. "Don't you?"

"Things look pretty bleak at the moment."

He passed the ladle to Reggie. "They always do. That's what makes the sun bursting through the clouds all the more beautiful."

"Tell us about this stolen-identity thing," Reggie said. "Are you sure it's you and not some other Marcy Singer?"

"Positive." I explained how I got my first clue from Julie and then how Alfred had confirmed it earlier today.

"That's scary," Reggie said. "Will you have to pay anything back?"

"I don't know. I canceled my credit cards and notified the bank. Alfred is doing some further investigating."

"Do you think someone found financial documents in your garbage?" Manu asked.

"No. I always shred documents before putting them in the trash," I said.

"That's good," Manu said.

"Not necessarily." Reggie took a cheese biscuit and passed the basket to me. "If the information wasn't taken from Marcy's garbage, then where did the identity thief get it?"

"Good point," Manu said. "Did this happen just after your arrival here in Tallulah Falls?"

I took a biscuit and placed it on my plate beside the soup bowl. "Actually, given the date of the illegal usage, it must have happened before I got here."

"Could it have been an online transaction?" Reggie asked.

"I don't think so. The transaction was with a real estate company," I said. "And I didn't even search online sites for property here. Sadie saw that the shop was available, and she set me up with a Realtor who helped me find the house."

Manu and Reggie shared a look.

"Bill Trelawney," Manu said. "We know he was involved with Four Square. It's likely he's the one who stole your information."

"But how does this affect my credit and reputation in Tallulah Falls?" I asked. "Do I have other bad debts floating around?"

"Call Vera," Reggie said, dipping a piece of her biscuit into her bowl of chowder. "Her husband, John, is the president of the Tallulah Falls bank branch. He'll be able to help you sort everything out."

"Thanks, Reggie. I'll do that."

After we ate our dinner, I let Angus back inside. He greeted the Singhs and then wandered into the living room with us and lay down by the fire.

Reggie opened the ledger and placed it on the table in front of the sofa. She, Manu, and I gathered around it to see what we could make of it.

"I agree this must be a dummy ledger," Manu said. "There's no logical flow of information here."

"Right. And before I came across this one," Reggie said, "I thumbed through two or three of Bill's other ledgers. They were perfectly organized and made perfect sense."

Manu nodded. "Yes, but this one made

perfect sense, too. To Bill."

"So we need to figure out his thought process when he compiled this information," I said.

There were months written in the columns at the top of the page. There were five of them: April, July, October, December, and February.

"We could start by determining the significance of these months," I said. "Could these represent his favorite holidays? April for Easter, July for Independence Day, October for Halloween, December for Christmas, and February for Valentine's Day?"

"Easter sometimes comes in March," Reggie pointed out.

"True," I said. "Maybe Mr. Trelawney's birthday was in April."

"I guess it's worth looking into," Manu said. "But it still doesn't tell us how the months relate to the names and figures in the columns below them."

At that point, I was at a complete loss. If we couldn't even figure out why Mr. Trelawney had designated the months at the top columns of his ledger the way he had, how could we possibly begin to break whatever code held the secrets to this ledger?

"Look," Reggie said, pointing to a name

near the end of the first page. "Timothy Enright. And there's a *b* beside his name."

"Do you think that means Timothy Enright was a straw buyer?" I asked.

"If he was, it never came out in court," Manu said.

"Neither did Four Square's silent partner," Reggie said.

Manu inclined his head. "You've got me there. Let's agree for now that the *b* notations do indicate straw buyers. Timothy lost his business, and Lorraine says the well has run dry. Where is his compensation for acting as a straw buyer for Four Square?"

"Maybe he invested it elsewhere or put it into an account his wife didn't know about," I said.

"But what about the business?" Reggie asked.

"Maybe he didn't lose it," I said. "Maybe he was simply tired of it."

She shrugged. "Maybe. It's possible that he was tired of the business and Lorraine and wanted to start all over without either one of them."

She turned the page, running her finger down the names to see if any more of them were familiar. It wasn't long before she came across another one.

She looked at me and frowned.

"What is it?" I asked.

"Todd Calloway," she said, "with a *b.*"

"Todd? A straw buyer?" I turned from Reggie to Manu. "You don't think that's true, do you?"

"Once again, his name didn't turn up in any of the paperwork." Manu bit his lip. "But his name is in this ledger for some reason."

Todd wasn't the only surprise we got. Blake's name was in there, too. And so was mine.

My jaw dropped when I saw my name on the ledger. I turned to look at Reggie and Manu, and they were as shocked as I was.

"M-maybe this isn't a dummy ledger after all," I said. "Maybe it's merely a list of Mr. Trelawney's renters."

"Had you paid Mr. Trelawney twenty-two thousand dollars, Marcy?" Manu asked.

I shook my head. We all sat quietly digesting this new information for a minute.

"What does this mean?" I finally asked.

"My best guess," Manu said with a sigh, "is that all these people had their identities stolen by Mr. Trelawney."

I grabbed my cordless phone. "Let me call Blake and see if he knows anything."

I dialed the MacKenzies' number as

Reggie and Manu continued to study the ledger.

"Blake," I said when he answered, "has your identity been stolen?"

"Is this a joke?"

"No. I'm serious. I found out a little while ago that my identity was stolen. Reggie discovered a ledger at Mr. Trelawney's house."

"You mean, of our rent?"

"No, it's a dummy ledger. We're afraid Mr. Trelawney might've been giving our financial information to Four Square for some sort of kickback."

"What makes you think that?"

"Well, as I said, I learned my identity was stolen, and my name is here in this ledger. It's marked with a notation Manu, Reggie, and I believe means 'straw buyer.' And, Blake, your name is in here, too."

"You say Manu is there?"

"Yes. Do you need to speak with him?"

"No . . . no. I've . . . uh . . . I have to go right now, Marcy."

"Wait. You need to check your credit report and see if your credit has been compromised. I —"

"Yeah, I'll do that. Thanks."

With that, he hung up. And for some reason, a chill ran down my spine.

CHAPTER THIRTEEN

I turned off the phone, and Reggie and Manu looked at me expectantly.

"He . . . said he'll . . . he'll check it out," I told them.

Manu nodded. "That's good. In the meantime, I'll give this ledger to the chief."

I was relieved when Manu and Reggie stood up to leave. They thanked me for dinner, and we exchanged good-byes with promises to keep one another posted on any progress we made deciphering the ledger information.

I locked the door, turned off the lights, and headed upstairs as soon as the Singhs left. I ran a tub filled with foamy, aromatic bubbles. As I sank into the tub, I thought about Mr. Trelawney. He'd seemed like such a sweet old guy. I hated the thought of him stealing my identity.

I placed a warm washcloth over my face and lay back against the tub.

Why had Blake acted so strangely? Was it possible he'd been making dinner or attending to his sick wife, and my call had simply caught him off guard? But then why had he asked about Manu? And why did I have the horrible suspicion that he'd done something he didn't want Manu to know about? Had he, in fact, acted as a straw buyer for Mr. Trelawney?

I'd trusted Sadie with the financial information she needed to act on my behalf so I wouldn't have to make numerous visits to and from Tallulah Falls until everything was finalized. Had Blake used that information to my detriment? That thought was even more disturbing than the thought of Mr. Trelawney misusing my financial information.

The phone rang, but I was too comfortable to get out of the tub and race to the bedroom to answer it. Whoever it was could leave a message. It was probably Mom. I only hoped Alfred hadn't told her about the identity theft. It would worry her silly, and there wasn't a thing that could be done at this time that Alfred wasn't already doing. Alfred could fix anything . . . well, almost.

When I got out of the bathtub, I put on my robe and slippers and padded to the bedroom. Angus had already commandeered the bed. I nudged him slightly to make him give me some room, and he moved aside.

I pressed the button on the answering machine.

A harsh voice whispered, "What does Margaret Trelawney know?" I couldn't be sure, but it sounded as if a man had made the call.

I grabbed the phone and dialed the number required to see where the call had originated.

The mechanical voice informed me, "The last number that called your line is not known."

When the phone rang again, I was hesitant to answer it. But part of me knew that if I didn't answer and it was the same person who had called before, he'd just keep calling. Besides, maybe I could reason with him.

After the third ring, I picked up the receiver. "Hello." I tried not to sound afraid.

"What does Margaret Trelawney know?" the voice asked in a gruff whisper.

"Excuse me?" I asked. "Who's calling?"

"What does she know?"

"I have no idea what you're talking about," I said, proud that I was able to keep the tremor out of my voice.

The line went dead.

I hung up the phone and realized I was shaking. Angus whimpered.

"Come here, baby," I said. "Come here."

He crawled around until the top half of his body was lying across my lap. I wrapped my arms around his neck and buried my face in his fur.

"It's okay," I said softly. "It's okay."

I wasn't sure if I was trying to reassure him or myself.

It hadn't been five minutes before the phone rang again. Once again, I hesitated, then answered.

"Hello." My voice wasn't as confident as it had been before.

"Hey, Marcy, it's Blake. Still got company?"

"No."

"Great, have you got a sec?"

"Sure. Is everything okay with Sadie?"

"Oh yeah. She's home — went to bed early. I'm out running a couple errands for the shop."

I digested this in silence.

"Anyway, I just wanted to call and thank you for letting me know about the stolen-identity thing. I'm sorry that happened to you, but our credit is fine."

"Oh. That's good."

"Yeah. Um . . . about that ledger . . . Do

you still have it?"

"No. Manu took it with him. He's going to pass it along to Chief Myers."

"Huh. Did you guys come to any conclusions about it?"

"Not yet."

"Look, Marcy, I know why my name is on that list."

"Then please explain it to me, because my name is in there, too."

"Please don't say anything to Sadie, okay? Promise?"

I paused, a bad feeling settling in my stomach. "Okay."

"Or Manu, either. Seriously, Marcy, promise me."

"All right. I promise."

"See, a while back, I was behind in my rent. I'd been renovating the house — you know, now that Sadie and I are ready to start a family, right?"

"Right."

"And I asked Mr. Trelawney to cut me a break on that month's rent because we'd be getting our income-tax refund soon and I'd pay him then."

"What did Sadie think about that?" I asked.

"She didn't know. She thought I was able to spend money on the house because we'd

215

had a really good month at the shop. That was partly true, but as I suspect you know, a few hundred bucks doesn't go very far when you're renovating your house."

"So you used your rent money."

"And some money from savings. I kept intending to put it all back as soon as that refund money came in. But when our accountant prepared our returns, we wound up owing money. We hadn't paid enough on our estimated tax payments."

"What did you tell Mr. Trelawney?"

Blake blew out a long breath. "See, that's the thing. By the time I found out we owed money to the government, I was more than one month behind in the rent."

"How much more?"

"Three months. So I went to Mr. Trelawney and explained the situation . . . and he was really cool about it. He said he'd wipe the past three months' debt out altogether and we'd start over fresh on one condition."

"That you become a straw buyer for Four Square," I said.

"Not even that," he said. "He just asked if he could use my financial information to make a transaction. I asked if I'd get in any trouble over it, and he promised I wouldn't. And I didn't."

"You didn't even ask what kind of transaction?"

"The man was offering to wipe out three months' rent, Marcy. If I wasn't getting in trouble over it, I didn't care."

"Then how do you know that isn't on your credit history?"

"Because it was never filed," Blake said. "It never came up, and I never questioned it."

"Not even after the Four Square people went to jail?"

"This happened after that. Look, Marcy, I'm counting on you not to tell Sadie or Manu or Chief Myers about any of this. It's not that a big a deal. The old man wanted to use my financial information for some reason and was willing to wipe out a substantial debt for the privilege. As long as I wouldn't get in trouble, I didn't care what he did with it."

"So what about me? Why am I in the ledger?"

"I don't know. Maybe he needed someone else's information and borrowed yours, not thinking it would get out of hand or that you'd ever know." He blew out another breath. "I'm sorry you got in the middle of this. Can I count on you to keep my name out of it?"

"As far as I'm concerned, you can. But Manu has already seen your name in the ledger. He might question you about it."

"Well, at least I'll be prepared if that does happen."

"You might want to talk it over with Sadie before that happens," I said. "She'll be awfully hurt if she finds it out from Manu."

"Yeah, I know. Thanks again. And good night."

"Good night, Blake."

I hung up the phone and lay my head back against the pillows. What a mess. How on earth could Blake let himself become involved in this?

For some strange reason, I impulsively picked up the phone and dialed the number to find out where the call from Blake had originated.

The mechanical voice droned, "The last number that called your line is not known."

I knew I should call the police and report the harassing calls, but I didn't. What if it *had been* Blake? He'd never hurt me. He'd just gotten himself into a mess and didn't know how to get out of it. I didn't want to be the reason my best friend's husband got arrested and thrown in prison for who knows how long.

"Thanks for ruining our lives, Marce,"

Sadie would say. "It's not like *you've* never made a mistake."

I slept that night better than I'd expected and was happy to see there were a couple of boxes sitting by the front door when I got to work the next day. For some reason, most of my shipments arrive on Saturday.

I was expecting some Pacific Coast Collage design packs by Laura J. Perin from Nordic Needle. The collages were beautiful, and perfect for those of us living here on the Oregon coast. They were sure to be a hit with my customers.

The design had an otter in the middle of the canvas, surrounded by blocks containing shells, a butterfly, a starfish, and other patterns. The design pack even came with bead packs and a shell to be placed between the otter's paws. I was planning on starting on my own Pacific Coast Collage to frame and display in the shop after I finished the tote bag, the MacKenzies' Mochas logo, and the haunted house. I know, I know; I always have too many projects going at once. But that's better than not having a project at all.

Thinking of the MacKenzies' Mochas logo brought to mind Blake's phone call. I still couldn't understand how he could let himself get involved in Mr. Trelawney's shady dealings. Nor could I understand how my own name had wound up on that list and my credit history compromised.

And what about Todd? Had he, like Blake, allowed Mr. Trelawney to use his financial information? Had he simply been a pawn like me? Or had he actually been a straw buyer for Four Square Development and had avoided detection?

I opened the top box and was delighted to see that it did, in fact, contain my Pacific Coast Collage design packs. I looked at the photograph of the completed collage, particularly the otter's sweet face.

I had thought I'd love life here in Tallulah Falls. And for the first month, it had held such promise. Now I was wondering if I ever should have left San Francisco.

I'd wanted to embark on an adventure, but this was ridiculous.

I was putting the Pacific Coast Collage design packs — all but one — on display when the bell over the door jingled. I looked up to see Vera.

I smiled. "Good morning. You're here early."

"I know. John went in to the bank this morning, and for some reason, I didn't want to be home alone." She gave me a half smile. "I suppose it's all the craziness that's been going on lately. How's Margaret?"

"Pretty good, I think. She left yesterday to stay with Sylvia in Portland for a few days."

"Oh, that's good."

Angus brought his tennis ball and dropped it at Vera's feet.

She laughed. "You're feeling friskier than I am this morning, my good man." She tossed the ball, and Angus loped after it.

"Look what I just got in," I said, showing her one of the collages.

She took in a breath. "How beautiful. I want one. Do you think I can do that?"

"You can do anything you put your mind to," I said, thinking that I'd help her through the hard parts. "By the way, I heard yesterday afternoon that my identity was stolen."

"You're kidding!"

"I wish I were. Do you think John could see me about it sometime this week?"

"You can see him today," she said, taking her cell phone out of her purse. She walked over to the sitting area and set down her tote as she called her husband. "John, darling, it's Vera. Someone has stolen our Marcy's identity."

Our Marcy. That made me smile.

I'd been so impressed with the collages, I hadn't opened the other box yet. The collages were the only things I'd been expecting, so I was curious about the other box. The return address was unfamiliar. And it wasn't from the East, so it couldn't be that Mom was sending me something from New York or somewhere.

In the background, I could hear Vera talking with John. I took my scissors and cut the tape binding the box. When I opened the top, I saw nothing but newspaper at first. I began taking out the newspaper and saw that inside the box was a bees' nest.

A hornets' nest, to be exact.

CHAPTER FOURTEEN

Vera approached me, returning her cell phone to her purse. "Okay, he —" She broke off and placed her hand gently on my forearm. "Are you all right? You're as white as rice."

"I'm . . . I'm fine. I just wasn't expecting . . . that."

Vera peered into the box and gasped. "What on God's green earth is that thing? A bees' nest?"

I nodded. "I believe it's supposed to be symbolic."

"If one of your beaus is trying to tell you he wants to be your honey," she said with a grimace, "he's going about it in an entirely creepy way."

I grinned. "What were you going to say before?"

"Oh, that John can see us now if we go on over."

"Great."

I set the box containing the hornets' nest in the storeroom. I'd go by the police station on my way back here to see if someone could come to the shop and take a look at it. Maybe whoever had sent it had left fingerprints on the box. But somehow I doubted it. I agreed with Vera — it certainly was creepy.

I kissed Angus on the top of the head and told him to be a good boy for the few minutes I'd be gone. Then I put one of those clock signs on the door saying when I'd be back and locked the door. I didn't expect to be gone more than half an hour.

"Shall we take my car?" Vera asked, indicating a silver BMW. "I still plan on stitching when we're finished talking with John."

It wouldn't make sense to take two cars, but I couldn't impose on Vera to drive me to both the bank and the police station. I decided a call to the police station would serve as well as a visit.

I smiled. "Sure."

For the second time in as many days, I was not in the driver's seat. I had to admit, though, I didn't feel in control of anything at all at the moment.

John Langhorne's office was weird. I suppose a more politically correct person would call it idiosyncratic. I'm sticking with *weird.*

It rather reminded me of one of those online games where you study a scene and find the hidden objects. To say Mr. Langhorne's desk was cluttered was akin to saying the Grand Canyon was a big hole.

Both an in-box and an out-box were filled with loose papers and files. Files, yellow legal pads, at least two pencil cups jammed full of pens and pencils, a tape dispenser, a large stapler, a mini stapler, various stamps, a bottle of rubbing alcohol, a bottle of hand sanitizer, and a tube of hand cream crowded the desk. A credenza behind the desk contained various alcoholic beverages, seltzer, and bottled water, a coffee urn and a teapot (both of which sat on a hot plate). Assorted cups, mugs, and glasses took up the rest of that space. A side table situated between the desk and the credenza provided the only apparent workspace, complete with desk, mouse, and keyboard.

The aesthetic pieces were strange, too. Instead of austere "banker" scenes or Norman Rockwell prints, Mr. Langhorne's office contained surrealist paintings. Not like Dalí or Escher, but like . . .

"Wow, did you do these paintings yourself?" I asked.

"He didn't," Vera said, "but I did." She

smiled smugly, obviously proud of her work.

"Wow," I repeated.

"And now my little artist has applied her talents to the embroidery canvas," Mr. Langhorne said, rising from his gray leather desk chair to give his wife a peck on the cheek. "Isn't she prolific?"

"Indeed," I said.

"Vera tells me you've been the victim of identity theft," he said, sitting back down and indicating that we do likewise. "I'm terribly sorry to hear that. How can I help?"

"Mainly, Mr. Langhorne, I want to check to make sure that, other than this bogus real estate transaction, my credit history is good. After all, this bank holds the mortgage to my home."

Mr. Langhorne bobbed his small, balding head. "No red flags have come across my desk. Of course, I wasn't aware of the real estate transaction. What's that about?"

I explained about my call from Alfred.

Mr. Langhorne frowned. "That's disturbing. I'll do a quick search later this afternoon, and I'll be sure to let you know if anything else shows up. I'm sure your attorney is doing thorough credit checks, as well." He shook his head. "Hopefully, this was merely an unfortunate accident. Transposed numbers do happen . . . more often than people think, actually."

"True, but, Mr. Langhorne, the transactions were in *my name.*"

"Ah yes . . . Well, let me look into it further, and I'll let you know if I find something. All right?"

"Sure." I stood. "Thank you for your time."

"Anytime," he said. "You ladies enjoy your stitching. Vera, darling, I'll see you at dinner."

Vera and her husband shared another quick kiss, and then she and I returned to the shop.

She settled onto the sofa to work on her tote bag while I took Angus for a bathroom break. I used that opportunity to call Detective Nash.

"Ted Nash," he answered.

"Good morning, Detective," I said. "It's Marcy Singer. I wondered if you or one of your officers could bring your handy-dandy fingerprinting kit over here and check out a box for me."

"A box? Should I bring the bomb squad?"

"No, I've already opened it."

"Marcy, you should never open a suspicious box."

"It didn't look suspicious. It still doesn't. It's the hornets' nest inside the box that bothers me."

"Is it full of hornets?"

"I don't think so. At least, none swarmed out when I opened the box."

"Where's the box now?"

"In the storeroom."

"Good. I'll be right over, and I'll bring a couple crime-scene techs with me."

After talking with Detective Nash, Angus and I returned to the shop. I retrieved my tote bag and went to sit by Vera. I had the top third of Angus' head completed on my tote bag, and Vera's teacup was looking more like a teacup every minute.

She looked up from her work and smiled. "John's probably right about this identity-theft thing being a misunderstanding. I'd rather think that than believe someone did this to you on purpose. Wouldn't you?"

"I would rather think that, yes." The trouble was, I didn't think that.

When Detective Nash, a young man, and a woman who appeared to be in her mid-forties arrived, I escorted them to the storeroom. Detective Nash introduced me to the man and woman as Scott and Shirley, crime-scene technicians who could analyze any trace evidence found on the suspicious box. I left them to their task and placed Angus in the bathroom until the techs could obtain whatever they needed.

"Is this about the bees' nest?" Vera asked when I returned to the sitting area.

I nodded.

"Somebody wants to impress his lady friend," she said in a singsong voice and with an eyebrow raised in Ted Nash's direction.

I shrugged, not quite knowing how to respond to that.

She saw that her thread had become too short to go any farther, so she ran the thread through some stitches on the back of the pattern and then cut it off. As she rethreaded her needle, she cocked her head. "On the other hand, you may not want to settle down with a lawman. That's dangerous work. Of course, your pub owner could become too fond of the drink. I've seen liquor ruin many a good man."

I remembered Mr. Langhorne's credenza and wondered if that could apply to him, but I kept my mouth shut.

At that moment, Detective Nash called me into the storeroom . . . an act for which I will be forever grateful.

"Any idea where this box came from?" he asked.

"Not really. Mr. Patrick warned me about stirring up hornets' nests, but I seriously doubt this came from the prison. Still, I'll mention it to Riley Kendall and see what sort of reaction I get."

He nodded. "We're going to take this back to the station, if that's all right with you."

"Suits me," I said. "I haven't had enough time to get sentimentally attached to it yet."

He rolled his eyes. "I'll check back with you later. In the meantime, don't open any suspicious boxes."

After Vera and the police left, I called Riley Kendall and asked if she could come by the shop today. She said she was in her office but would be leaving at lunchtime.

"Would you like me to bring something for us to eat while we chat?" she asked. "I'm craving Captain Moe's ham and Swiss on rye."

"Captain Moe?"

Riley laughed. "Yup. It's a deli this side of Depoe Bay. Captain Moe is the owner. He's this jolly bear of a man who reminds everyone of Santa Claus. Actually, he always plays Santa in the Tallulah Falls Christmas parade."

"Why does he call himself Captain Moe?" I asked.

"He's an actual captain. He used to pilot a salmon boat. I'll run by there and then come on over. Is ham and Swiss on rye all right with you, or would you like something else?"

"Ham sounds delicious. Thank you."

When I ended the call, I marveled at how cheerful Riley had sounded. I'd never heard her that way before. Was there a reason for this bubbly new attitude? Or was it an act?

Riley arrived at the shop about forty-five minutes after we'd spoken. She carried a white bag bearing Captain Moe's logo: a likeness that reminded me not so much of Santa Claus as of Alan Hale Jr. as the Skipper on *Gilligan's Island,* only with a beard. Captain Moe was tipping his hat and smiling jovially from the bag.

The contents of the bag smelled divine, and Angus loped over with his nose in the air to greet Riley as soon as she walked in.

"I'm sorry," I said. "Let me put him in the bathroom while we have lunch." I snapped his leash onto his collar.

"Here," Riley said, reaching into the bag and pulling out a small sack. "I told Uncle Moe about Angus, and he sent a ham bone. I thought you might want to give it to the poor pup before shutting him away from us." She grinned. "Might make it a bit more palatable for him."

I agreed and thanked her for her thought-

231

fulness. Angus went far more willingly into the bathroom with the promise of his treat.

When I came back, I found that Riley had arranged our lunch on the coffee table and was sitting in front of it cross-legged on the floor. She'd taken a pillow from one of the navy sofas to prop against her back.

"I thought we could eat Japanese style, if that's okay. Or is it Chinese? I always forget."

"I know the Vietnamese sit on the floor while they eat."

"Either way, I figure I'd better take advantage of doing this while I still can." She smiled. "I found out yesterday that I'm having a girl."

"Congratulations! I didn't even know you were pregnant."

"Thank you, but I'm sure I won't be able to hide my burgeoning tummy for much longer. Now, let's eat, and you can tell me why you asked me to come by."

I sat on the floor on the other side of the table. "I got a strange . . . gift . . . in the mail today." I unwrapped my sandwich but kept my eyes on Riley's face. "It was a hornets' nest."

She frowned. "A hornets' nest? At least there weren't any hornets in it. Were there?"

"No. How did you know?"

"Because hornets are usually dead by this time of year. Entomology — along with apiology —"

At my blank expression, she explained, "The study of bees. It was my minor in college." She shrugged. "I've always been a bug girl. Do you know who might've sent it?" Realization dawned on her face. "Oh, I get it. Because Dad told you not to stir up any hornets' nests, right?"

"Right. I know your dad didn't send it — he couldn't have. But" — I bit my lower lip — "it had to be someone who knows he said that to me."

"There's more to this than you're telling me." She put down her sandwich. "Put some money on the table."

"Excuse me?"

"A twenty, a five, a one . . . whatever you have on you. Put it on the table."

I went to the office, took a twenty from my purse and sat it on the table beside Riley. "Now what?"

"Now you've hired me to act as your attorney. We have attorney-client confidentiality. Spill."

I closed my eyes.

"Can't help you if you won't let me, Marcy."

"If it wasn't your dad and it wasn't you,

233

doesn't it stand to reason that it was Todd, Blake, or Sadie?" I asked. "They were the only ones with me at the prison."

"Maybe so. But anyone who knows Dad knows he uses that expression fairly often. What makes you think it was one of your friends? Are you going mondo paranoid on me?"

"Both Blake and Todd were on a list kept by Mr. Trelawney. My name was on that list, as well, and I found out my identity was stolen."

"Ooh, too bad." She wiped her mouth with her napkin. "Want me to look into that for you?"

"Thanks, but my mom's attorney is handling it. Anyway, I called Blake to warn him that he, too, may be a victim of identity theft. He said not to tell the police or Sadie but that he'd allowed Mr. Trelawney to use his financial information in lieu of three months' rent."

Riley swallowed and wiped her mouth again. "That was dumb."

"I know. But get this: Before he called me and confided all that —"

"I thought you called him."

"I did, but he was noncommittal during that conversation and called me back later when he was out running errands."

"Ah, didn't want to talk in front of the wife. Gotcha."

"So before Blake called, I got two spooky calls asking me about what Margaret Trelawney knows."

Riley barked out a laugh. "That call shouldn't have taken long. I'm sorry. It's just that Mrs. T strikes me as a tad dotty. Why would someone call you to find out what she knows, anyhow?" She took another bite of her sandwich.

"Because Mrs. Trelawney thinks I'm the only one who agrees that her husband's murder and Timothy Enright's murder are connected, and she may have been spreading that all over town, for all I know."

"Oh yeah. Heard about the break-in. What then?"

I took a drink of my soda. "After receiving the call, I did a star-six-nine on my phone to see where the call had originated. I was told that the number wasn't known. I got the same message after doing a star-six-nine after Blake called."

Riley shook her head. "That's no big deal. Might just be a coincidence."

"I'm hearing the words *coincidence* and *misunderstanding* all over the place today. Isn't that a little too coincidental?"

"Not necessarily. Maybe you are just being a little paranoid. Heck, if a guy died in my storeroom one week and my landlord was shot to death the next, I'd probably be freaked myself."

Since Riley was halfway through her sandwich and I hadn't even tasted mine, I took a bite. It was quite good. There was a spicy honey mustard on the sandwich that gave it some zip.

"Do you still have that hornets' nest?" she asked.

I shook my head.

"You threw it away?"

I swallowed. "No. The police took it."

"If they give it back, can I have it?"

I grinned. "By all means. Do you think that's coincidental, too?"

"No. I think that one means something. I'm going up to visit Dad later. I'll get his input."

"Congratulate him for me on the grand-daughter."

She smiled. "I will." Her smile faded. "In the meantime, watch your back."

Long after Riley had left, I sat at the counter, looking out the window at the rain. I smiled slightly when I saw Detective Nash drive up. Hopefully, he'd learned something about my mysterious box. I noticed he wasn't carrying it.

He entered the shop and immediately rubbed his arms. "That's a cold rain."

"Don't make me dread leaving any more than I already do."

He arched a brow as a raindrop rolled down his cheek. "You dread leaving work? Are you afraid to go home?"

"No. Not really. I'm dreading going out in the rain, that's all."

"You said 'not *really.*' Are you afraid?"

"No," I said.

"Well, the hornets' nest came from a nature center in northern California. There was a tag underneath the nest and the return address turned out to be theirs, as well."

"So it *is* a coincidence? It was sent to me by mistake?"

"Hardly," Detective Nash said. "Someone claiming to be you — or to be calling on your behalf — called, ordered, and paid for the nest."

"Then you have a credit card receipt?"

"Yes, yours. But Manu told me about the identity theft. So, we've got nothing."

"There were no prints?"

He shook his head.

"I didn't really think there would be. But a girl can hope."

"It's okay," he said. "Someday your prints will come."

I closed my eyes. "That was terrible."

"I know it was lame, but it's the best I can do today." He smiled.

The shop bell jingled, and Todd Calloway walked in. "Hope I'm not interrupting official police business."

"Hi, Todd," I said.

"Calloway." The irritation in Detective Nash's voice was evident. I wondered if he resented the interruption or if he knew something about Todd that I didn't.

"I can go over here and look at embroidery thread or play with Angus, if you guys still have business to discuss," Todd said.

"It's all right," Detective Nash said. "I was on my way out. Marcy, you have my number."

"Right."

Detective Nash left, and a grinning Todd sidled up next to me. "I don't think he cares for me. At least, not as much as he cares for you."

I scoffed. "It truly was police business."

"Oh yeah? What's up?"

"I got a hornets' nest in the mail today."

"That's weird."

"Yeah, I know. So, what brings you by?"

"I took the evening off and wanted to

know if I could hang out with you and Angus, provided I bring a video, some popcorn, and a rawhide chew. That is, unless you have other plans . . . or some more official police business."

"No," I said after a pause. "Angus and I would be delighted to have you join us for the evening." I still wasn't quite sure what to think about the fact that his name was in the ledger, but I thought that this at least would give me an opportunity to feel him out on the subject. Plus, having a handsome, likable guy over for a movie wasn't much of a sacrifice.

I showered, changed clothes at least twice, and took extra time with my hair and makeup before Todd's arrival. Since we were having a casual evening, I wore jeans and a long-sleeved pale blue blouse. Though I longed to go barefoot, I slipped on black mules that I could easily step into or out of, making them the next best thing to being barefoot. I wore the diamond stud earrings Mom had given me for my twenty-first birthday. And I curled my hair so it would fall in tousled waves around my face.

After getting myself ready, I went to the kitchen to see what I could throw together in the way of appetizers. I studied the freezer, because that's where I keep most of my Unexpected Company Is Coming food-stuffs.

I had some mini bacon-and-cheddar quiches, which have the flakiest crusts ever. Plus, they have bits of onion that really enhance the flavor of the eggs. I was nearly drooling in anticipation as I preheated the oven.

I found a box of cheesecake bites that required nothing but thawing. I took them out and arranged them on a decorative plate. There were three flavors: key lime, strawberry, and triple chocolate. With Todd bringing the popcorn, I decided the cheese-cakes and quiches would be plenty.

I was taking the quiches out of the oven when the doorbell rang. "Coming," I called, setting the cookie sheet with the mini quiches on a trivet.

I hurried to the living room and opened the door. And to think I'd been drooling over quiches. Todd looked way better than the quiches and the cheesecakes combined.

He wore jeans and a black henley open at the throat. His dark hair glistened, and his eyes were that mixture of good-boy sweet-ness and bad-boy charm that makes a woman's heart drop to her knees. And he was carrying a bouquet of roses, daisies, and chrysanthemums. Now I ask you: Does it get any better than that?

He held out a rawhide bone. "This is for you." He inclined his head toward the flowers. "These are for Angus. Unless you two would prefer to swap."

"I believe we would," I said, taking the flowers.

Todd followed me into the kitchen. "Where is Angus?"

"He's in the backyard at the moment. I thought it would be best to let him in after we've had our fill of snacks."

"That's not a bad idea. I'd imagine our boy could take care of those quiches in about one gulp."

"Two, if he took time to chew. What movie did you bring?"

"I didn't. I did bring the popcorn, though."

I took a white vase from beneath the sink, filled it three-quarters of the way full of water, and arranged the bouquet in the vase.

"You take pains with everything you do, don't you?" Todd asked.

"I think if you're going to do something, you should do it right."

"Oh, I agree." A lazy smile played across his lips. "I agree wholeheartedly."

Something in the way he said that made me blush. I turned away so he couldn't see.

He laughed softly. Darn it; he'd seen.

I finished arranging the flowers, washed my hands, and put the quiches on a platter. I nodded toward the cheesecakes. "Can you get those?"

"Yes, ma'am."

We set the food on the coffee table and still had room for the tub of popcorn Todd had brought. I returned to the kitchen for plates, silverware, napkins, and drinks.

"You didn't bring any home brew tonight?" I asked with a grin as I handed Todd a soda.

"Not tonight. I wanted us to have clear heads." His voice turned serious. "I want to get to know you, Marcy."

"I want to get to know you, too."

"And I don't want either of us to have fuzzy tongues or fuzzy memories in the morning."

I burst out laughing, and so did he.

I waved my hand toward the food. "What will you have first?"

"This." He leaned toward me, raked his fingers through my hair, and pulled me to him for a deep, thorough kiss. Then he looked into my half-closed eyes for a moment before saying, "I've been wanting to do that for a long time. And now I think I'd better try a quiche."

At least, I think that's what he said. My mind had drifted back to the fantasy I'd ascribed to Vera in the store the other day where Todd had marched back into the shop, bent me over his arm, kissed me, and said, "You need to be kissed . . . often . . . and by someone who knows how." Boy, did he know how.

We made general small talk while we ate. But finally we were down to nibbling on the popcorn, and Angus was chewing on his rawhide at our feet. Unfortunately, our discussion was about to take a serious turn.

CHAPTER FIFTEEN

"How long have you known Blake and Sadie?" Todd asked.

"Sadie and I were roommates in college." I smiled. "Two nerdy girls. I was earning a bachelor's in business administration, with an emphasis in accounting, and Sadie was working toward her bachelor's in radiology."

"Radiology?"

"Yeah. She changed majors two or three times that first year. She went from radiology to communications." I raised my eyes to the ceiling and thought a second. "Then she switched to ecology, and finally wound up in hospitality management . . . where she stayed."

"And that gave her the skills she'd need for MacKenzies' Mochas," Todd said.

"Exactly. So, there you go. How about you? How long have you known the Mac-Kenzies?"

"About four years or so. In fact, it was

Blake who convinced me to open the Brew Crew."

"It was Sadie who convinced me to open the Seven-Year Stitch," I said with a laugh. "Those two are regular entrepreneur incubators."

"Yeah, it's a wonder they're not asking us for kickbacks."

The word *kickbacks* triggered thoughts of Bill Trelawney's ledger and the call I'd received from Blake last night.

"Did I say something wrong?" Todd asked. "You've gone all pensive on me all of a sudden."

"I was with Reggie Singh at the Trelawneys' house yesterday, and Reggie found a ledger. It was of particular concern to me because my name was in it."

"Why should that concern you? You rent from them just like I do, don't you?"

"That's the thing. It was a dummy ledger. There was a notation by my name — and the names of other people — that Reggie and Manu believe indicated the people were used as straw buyers. And I found out I've been the victim of identity theft."

Todd nodded slowly. "This has you thinking it was Bill Trelawney who stole your identity."

"Yes. And I should tell you — your name

is in the ledger, too."

He looked back at me stonily. I couldn't read him at all.

"Do you know why your name is in that ledger? Did Bill Trelawney ask you for a favor?" I asked.

"Nope." He looked at his watch. "I do know it's getting late, though. And as much as I've enjoyed our evening, I'd better be on my way."

"Are you sure?" I asked.

"Yeah." He gave me a half smile. In the light of the hallway, I could see lines from age — or worry — in the corners of his eyes.

I walked him to the door.

"You and Angus sleep tight tonight." He gave me a quick peck on the cheek and left.

I closed the door and went back to the sofa. As if sensing my bewilderment, Angus got up, walked over to me, and rested his head on my thigh. I absently scratched his head and wondered if I was the only person on that ledger who hadn't sold out to Bill Trelawney and Four Square Development.

Thankfully, the rest of the night was uneventful. The next morning, not wanting to take any chances with my only day off, I put Angus in the Jeep, and we left town right after breakfast.

We drove up the coast and parked at a secluded beach. Angus waded in the water, barked at birds and crabs, and dug in the sand. Like a mom overseeing her rowdy toddler, I sat on a lounge chair, reading a paperback and shouting seldom-heeded warnings. The wind was so gusty, I didn't dare take out the tote bag I'd hoped to work on. But overall, it was a pleasant morning, and just what I needed.

When I started getting hungry, Angus and I packed up and got back into the Jeep to go on a quest for lunch. I remembered Captain Moe's and decided to see if I could find the place.

It wasn't at all difficult to find. I began seeing billboards about seven miles out, and they led me straight to Captain Moe's. The diner seemed small on the outside but was roomier inside than I had thought it would be. The decor was either retro or old. Round swiveling stools on metal poles with red seats were lined up at a stainless-steel counter. Additional seating was provided by booths located against the walls. Like the stools, the booths featured red padding. The tables were white Formica with a metal base. Vintage metal signs and posters decorated the walls, and there was a jukebox in one corner. At the moment, the diner was empty.

"How can I help you, young lady?"

I turned to see Captain Moe himself coming through a set of double doors, a warm smile on his face.

"Hi," I said. "I'm Marcy Singer."

"Ah yes, Riley's friend. It's nice to meet you. Did you bring that wolfhound with you?"

"I did. He's waiting in the Jeep."

"Waiting in the Jeep? Well, go out there and get him."

"But won't your other patrons object?"

"What other patrons?" he asked. "Captain Moe's is closed on Sundays."

"Oh, I'm sorry," I said. "I'll come back another day."

"Nonsense. You're here; I'm here. I imagine you're hungry, or you wouldn't have come." He nodded toward the door. "Now go on out there and get that dog, and we'll have some lunch."

I hurried outside to get Angus. Upon entering the diner, Angus bounded over to Captain Moe as if the two were old friends. Maybe Captain Moe really was Santa Claus after all.

"Ah, you're a fine-looking lad," Captain Moe told Angus as the dog rolled over for a belly rub.

"Do you have any pets, Captain Moe?"

"Indeed I do. Four dogs and an ornery cat named Petey. They were all strays that came around looking for a handout and a bit of affection."

I smiled. "It appears they came to the right place."

"And yet here I am, flapping my jaws and letting you go hungry," he said. "What would you like for lunch?"

"Nothing," I said. "I'd feel horrible if I imposed on you like that."

"Then it's a good thing this is not an imposition. How about I fry the three of us up some cheeseburgers?"

"Cheeseburgers would be wonderful. Is there anything I can do?"

"Do you have any quarters on you?" he asked.

"I think so."

"Then get us some music to play on the jukebox. It's too quiet in here."

I went over to the jukebox and selected three of the most up-tempo tunes. Then, while Angus sniffed all around the dining room, I went into the kitchen to see if I could be of further assistance to Captain Moe.

He was standing at an industrial-size sink with his sleeves rolled up washing his hands and arms.

"Is there anything else I can do to help?"

"You can get washed up and get us some drinks, if you'd like. I'll have a root beer."

For some reason, I didn't feel odd in the least to be milling around the kitchen with this person I'd just met. I watched Captain Moe put three hamburger patties on the grill. The kitchen instantly filled with the sizzle and aroma of frying beef.

"Are you Santa Claus?" I asked. "Or an angel? Is this where I get the 'wonderful life' lesson?"

He laughed. And, in case you're wondering, it didn't sound like *Ho! Ho! Ho!* But it was close.

"I'm only an old man with a soft heart," he said. "When I came through those doors and into the diner, it was to tell whoever had come in that I was closed and only here doing inventory." He grinned. "But there you were . . . a wee stray looking lost and alone."

"Do I look that pitiful?" I asked with a laugh.

"Not pitiful." He flipped the burgers before turning to give me a fresh appraisal. "Sad. As if you're carrying the weight of the world on those tiny shoulders."

Tears pricked my eyes, but I blinked them

away. "I didn't realize I was that transparent."

"Like I said, I'm old. Besides, I've always been a good listener, so I've come to know certain signs."

"Signs?"

"Of sadness, despair, love, happiness. Maybe I should have been a bartender."

"Or a therapist," I said.

"They're not the same?" he asked, taking the burgers off the grill and placing two of them on sesame seed buns.

"Practically. But tending bar doesn't pay as well."

"You have a point." He added cheese to our burgers. "Would you like the works?"

"Please."

The works consisted of tomato, onion slices, pickles, lettuce, and generous dollops of both mayonnaise and mustard.

We started into the dining room, and I nearly tripped over Angus, who'd been smelling the frying burgers from beneath the door. I sat at the counter, and Captain Moe presented Angus with his burger on a paper plate before joining me at the counter. Before we ate, Captain Moe bowed his head and said grace.

We ate in silence for a moment. I, for one, was savoring my burger. Angus had already

251

Hoovered his and was staring at me with pleading eyes. I was trying to ignore him.

"Would you like to talk over what's troubling you?" Captain Moe asked. "Sometimes it helps to lay it all out where you can see it better."

So I did. I don't know quite what came over me, but I did. I told him about the move, Timothy Enright, Mr. Trelawney, Lorraine, Mrs. Trelawney, and Sylvia. . . . I even found myself telling Captain Moe about Mr. Trelawney's ledger and the names it contained.

Captain Moe let me ramble until I told him about the weird way the columns were separated by five random months.

"I think I might know what the months mean," he said.

"Really?" I asked. "Is it some nautical thing?"

He shook his head. "It might be birthday months. Unless you had two people whose birthdays fell in the same month, that would be a great way to keep track of disbursements among a few people without actually naming names."

"How clever," I said. "I'll ask one of the policemen to check and see if any of the Four Square people's birthdays were in the months used to head up the columns."

"Was one of the months December?"

"Yes, it was. How did you know?"

"I didn't know, but it was a practical guess in putting my theory to the test. My brother was a member of Four Square Development, and his birthday is in December."

"Your brother?"

He nodded. "Norm Patrick."

My jaw dropped. "Um . . . I . . . I didn't realize. . . ." I grabbed my purse. "I'd better go, Mr. — um . . . Captain — Moe. I've taken up too much of your time already."

"Come back anytime," he said.

At the shop Monday morning, I sat in my red chair, working on my tote bag. The bell jingled, and I looked over my shoulder to see Detective Nash walk in.

"Hello, Detective," I said, returning to my cross-stitching.

"Are you upset with Angus for some reason?"

"No, but it's such a nice day, I let him stay home in the backyard."

"I wasn't talking about his absence," Detective Nash said. "I was talking about the way you're stabbing the needle into that depiction of his face." He sat down on the sofa.

With a sigh, I set my work on the arm of

253

the chair. "I'm such an idiot."

"It was only one date," he said, wrinkling his nose in distaste. "And the way he barged in here probably caught you completely off guard. Stop beating yourself up over it."

"That's not what I'm beating myself up over. How did you know I had a date with Todd, anyhow?"

"Isn't that what he was doing here on Saturday?"

"Well, yes, but —"

"What are you beating yourself up over?"

"Yesterday I spilled my guts to Captain Moe. And then he told me he's Norman Patrick's brother. I mean, when I thought about it, Riley did call him Uncle Moe at one point the other day; but I thought she simply misspoke, or it was a friendly nickname. I didn't think he was actually her uncle."

"And?"

"And how could I be so foolish? I fell for Captain Moe's bighearted Santa routine and told him everything I know about the Trelawney case."

"Once again, I don't see the problem," Detective Nash said. "Captain Moe's bighearted Santa routine isn't a routine. He's a genuinely nice guy."

"But now Norman Patrick and who knows

who else knows everything I know."

"Captain Moe probably knew more about the case than you did to begin with. Everybody knows him, and everybody talks to him."

"I still can't believe I was stupid enough to speak of this to someone simply because he was nice to me, looked like Santa Claus, and made me a cheeseburger."

"He made you a cheeseburger? At the diner?"

I nodded.

"But Captain Moe's is closed on Sundays. No exceptions." He took a moment to reflect on this. "You must've been really pitiful."

"Thank you ever so much."

He spread his hands. "Hey, I'm just saying." He frowned slightly. "Then you were at the diner and didn't make the connection between Maurice Patrick and Norman Patrick?"

"Who's Maurice Patrick?"

"Captain Moe," he said, slapping his hand to his head. "It's right there on the business license, which is framed and hanging next to the coatrack by the door. Proprietor, Maurice Patrick."

I glared at him. "Who reads business licenses?" Before he could answer, I continued. "Other than you?"

"Look, it's really not a big deal that you talked with Captain Moe. He's a good guy, and he's fairly insightful. Did he give you any advice?"

"Well, he did provide a possible clue about Mr. Trelawney's ledger. He said the months could represent the birthdays of the people involved." I plucked a stray gray thread from my white sweater. "And he told me Norman Patrick's birthday is in December. I called and left a message on Reggie's voicemail yesterday telling her to tell Manu he might want to check the birthdates and ledger amounts to see how they correspond to the information he has on Four Square."

"Good," Detective Nash said. "I hope it can bring us closer to solving this case." He looked down at the rug. "I'd hate to see you give up everything you've worked this hard for and go back to San Francisco."

"You've been talking with Reggie?"

"Yes. She's worried about you, and she's hounding her husband and me to solve this case quickly, despite the fact that Chief Myers thinks it's all a waste of time."

"Is that why you stopped by? To put on your deer-stalker hat and revisit the crime scene with your trusty magnifying glass?"

"No, I came by to tell you we got the

autopsy report back on Timothy Enright. The cause of death was listed as alcohol poisoning."

"You mean, he wasn't poisoned? He was drunk after all?"

"It appears that way."

"You don't sound convinced."

"It doesn't matter whether or not I'm convinced. The case is officially closed."

CHAPTER SIXTEEN

Riley came in at lunchtime, still radiant and happy. "Hey, Marcy," she called as she entered the shop. "Do you have any baby stuff?"

I got up from behind the counter, where I'd been eating my lunch — peanut butter crackers and a diet soda. "I have lots of baby stuff. What, in particular, are you looking for?"

"Oh, you know: bibs, blankets — the whole nine."

"What's your embroidery specialty?" I asked.

"Retail. I want my baby to have lots of adorable hand-stitched things made just for her."

"But you don't do embroidery."

"Exactly." She smiled as if pleased that I finally got it. "I want you to make them for me. You've got plenty of time — a little more than five months. Will you do it? I'll pay you well."

"Sure, but bear in mind that I might not be able to get a really intricate, detailed project done before the baby gets here."

"That's all right," she said, "but let's see what we wind up with before making a timeline."

"Did you tell your dad this weekend that it's a girl?" I asked as I led Riley over to the cross-stitch bibs and baby-pattern books.

"I did. He's absolutely over the moon. I heard you paid a visit to Uncle Moe."

"Yeah. I hadn't really taken in the fact he's your uncle."

"Um . . . the *Uncle Moe* didn't tip you off?" She grinned. "He did say you were pretty blown away by that. He also said you didn't stay long after you found out we're related." She picked up a bib kit that had a sleepy teddy bear on the front. "How sweet is this? Anyway, he asked if you and I were on good terms, and I told him you don't quite trust me yet." She handed me the kit. "I definitely want this one."

"Why do you say that?" I asked.

"What? That you don't trust me? You don't. Not that I blame you. We didn't get off to the best of starts." She handed me another bib kit. This one had a baby duck with a fork in one winglike hand and a spoon in the other.

We then took a stack of pattern books over to the sofa so Riley could be comfortable as she perused them. The rest of our conversation consisted of exclamations of "How cute" and "Isn't this precious?" By the time Riley had finished looking through the pattern books, I'd agreed to make her the two bib kits, five additional bibs, and one small blanket.

We were finishing up when Lorraine Enright stormed into the shop.

"My husband's death has been ruled an accident," she said. "Can you believe it? An accident."

"I heard," Riley said. "I got a call from the chief this morning and was planning on calling you this afternoon. If you'll bring any insurance policies and leave them at the front desk, I can get started filing those claims for you."

"This isn't about insurance," Lorraine said, her face even redder than her hair. "This is about the fact that no one, like her" — she threw a venomous glance in my direction — "is paying for my husband's death."

"He is," Riley said. "And if it was — as the coroner's report indicates — an accident, then no one else is at fault."

"Someone forced Timothy to drink," Lorraine said. "I know they did. That or else he didn't know what he was drinking."

Riley handed me the pattern books and stood. "Come with me back to the office," she said gently to Lorraine. "I don't have any appointments until two p.m., and we can talk until then." She looked at me. "Thanks, Marcy. I'll talk with you in a day or two."

Sadie came over after MacKenzies' Mochas' lunch rush. She looked pale and thin, and I could see she was still weak.

"Hi," I said. "Glad to see you're up and about." I jerked my head toward the sofa. "Why don't you lie down and take a quick nap?"

"Really?" she asked, sitting on the edge of the sofa that faced away from the window. "You don't think anyone will mind?"

"I don't. Jill, do you mind?" I looked toward the mannequin. "Jill doesn't mind. And I don't see anyone else in the shop except you."

She took off her shoes and lay down. "This feels heavenly." She closed her eyes. "Blake told me about the deal he made with Mr. Trelawney."

"Did he?" I threaded black embroidery

floss through the eye of my needle.

"Yes. He told me you convinced him to tell me before Manu did. Thanks for that."

"You're welcome." I almost didn't say any more — didn't want to run the risk of kicking up any marital strife. But after a few stitches, I said, "It was completely by accident that I found out. I saw Blake's name in the ledger and was afraid you guys had been victims of identity theft, as I had."

"Blake talked with Manu about it."

"Is he in any trouble?"

"No."

I released a breath I didn't realize I'd been holding.

"Manu said that since Blake hadn't benefited from the fraudulent transaction," Sadie continued, "he isn't liable for what Mr. Trelawney did with the information. Plus, based on your situation, there's evidence to support the fact that Mr. Trelawney would've used the information whether he had Blake's permission or not."

"Thank goodness," I said. "I was afraid Blake might be forced to pay some sort of restitution or something."

"No. What my husband did was incredibly stupid, but not criminal."

"That tone tells me you haven't entirely forgiven him yet."

"I've forgiven him," she said, "but I'm still angry . . . and hurt. It bothers me that he wasn't honest with me from the beginning." She yawned. "I wouldn't have let Mr. Trelawney take advantage of him." She snuggled against one of the sofa cushions. "Did I mention how great this sofa feels?"

"You did. Go ahead and take your nap. If you're not awake by closing time, I'll either wake you up or lock you in here with Jill."

"Oh please, no." She shuddered. "That would completely freak me out. I'd begin having those Chucky-monster nightmares all over again. Remember how afraid I used to be of that stupid doll?"

"I do," I said, laughing. "I wouldn't have connected Jill to that thing, though. She is neither a redhead nor evil."

She giggled. "Yeah, yeah. Blondes have more fun and all that jazz."

"Precisely. We do have more fun, and that's why we aren't evil." I emphasized the *e* in *evil* and drew it out in my best Vincent Price voice . . . which wasn't much, but it worked. It made Sadie laugh.

Then she dozed off, and I continued working on my tote bag. For a little while, life seemed normal again.

As I arrived home that evening, my cell

phone started ringing in my bag. I juggled a few bags of groceries and managed to both keep them upright and answer it. It was Reggie.

"Your tip about the birthdays paid off," she said. "The column headings correspond to Four Square Development major players' birthday months."

"So what about the fifth?"

"That's what Manu is working on now. Today, he and some other officers — including a federal guy — went to talk with the men serving time in the Four Square case," she said. "They'll be asking about Bill Trelawney's role and what Timothy Enright might've meant about Four Square's fifth. I should know something tomorrow."

"Great. Keep me posted, will you?"

"I sure will."

After talking with Reggie, I unpacked the groceries, fed Angus, and made myself some chicken stir-fry and a salad. As I poured a glass of tomato juice and sat down to eat, I reflected on Lorraine Enright's outburst.

She was adamant that her husband hadn't drunk himself to death. I'd have been inclined to disagree before Bill Trelawney was murdered. Now I found myself agreeing with Lorraine. I came to the disturbing conclusion that Lorraine and I needed to compare notes.

I washed the dishes and straightened up the kitchen. I realized I was stalling, dreading making the attempt to speak rationally with Lorraine Enright. I picked up the phone book, half hoping Lorraine's number was unlisted. It wasn't.

I dialed the number. There was no answer, so I left a message.

"Hello, Lorraine. This is Marcy Singer. Like you, I don't believe Mr. Enright's death was accidental. I think someone is responsible, and I'd like to talk with you when —"

"I'm here," Lorraine said, picking up the receiver. "What gives? Why are you siding with me all of a sudden?"

"I've never intentionally sided against you," I said. "It seems to me that it's been the other way around."

"Why did you call me?"

"I don't know." I sighed. "I believe your husband's death and the murder of Bill Trelawney are somehow connected. And I thought if you and I could put our heads together, we might be able to figure out who'd want both of them dead."

She was so silent for so long, I started to think she'd hung up. Then she asked if she could come over.

It was a mild evening, so I put Angus in the backyard before Lorraine arrived. He'd never bitten anyone, but he was protective, and I didn't know how long a truce with Lorraine Enright could last.

I heard her car pull into the driveway about fifteen minutes after speaking with her by phone. I hadn't realized she lived that close. But Tallulah Falls is a small town. I suppose, in reality, everybody lives close to everybody here.

I invited her in and offered her a cup of decaffeinated coffee.

"I'd like that," she said, joining me in the kitchen.

I put the coffee on to brew, and then Lorraine and I sat down at the table.

"I was shocked when you called me," she said. "I mean, I have caller ID — which is why I didn't pick up right away. But when you started saying you believed me, I was surprised."

With an index finger, I traced the pattern on my ecru tablecloth. It was a Hardanger tablecloth. I'd made it as a housewarming present to myself. "I do think your husband's death and Mr. Trelawney's death are connected. I could be completely wrong, but —"

"No. No, I think so, too," she said. "I've

266

always thought that."

"What do you know about Four Square Development?"

"Not much. I know a bunch of people got caught up in some type of real estate fraud and went to jail. Riley's dad was one of them."

I got up to pour the coffee. "Reggie Singh found a ledger Mr. Trelawney had been keeping. The police are fairly certain it's a dummy ledger for Four Square." I placed the cups, spoons, sugar, and nonfat milk on the table and sat back down. "There were names in the ledger with notations thought to indicate straw buyers."

"Was Tim's name in the ledger?"

"Yes, and so was mine."

She paused with the sugar spoon halfway to her cup. "Your name was in it?"

I nodded. "Yesterday I learned I've been the victim of identity theft. We think Mr. Trelawney was using people's financial information — with or without their consent — for straw-buying purposes."

Lorraine continued putting sugar and milk into her coffee. "I suspect Mr. Trelawney had Tim's permission," she said quietly, as she stirred her coffee. "Our last fight was about Tim working on some type of partnership with Mr. Trelawney. I asked what it was all about, but Tim told me to wait and see." She placed her spoon on her napkin and sipped the coffee. "I kept waiting, but nothing ever happened."

"This was during the Four Square Development debacle?" I asked.

"No. It was shortly before Tim's death."

"What I can't understand is how Four Square Development was — or is — still operating with the four partners in prison," I said. "But your husband tried to scratch a message on my storeroom wall about Four Square's fifth. And I . . . well, I'm starting to think that maybe he wanted to talk with me because he knew my name was in that ledger."

"Today I took a look through Tim's papers, like I promised Riley, and it seems to me that Tim knew quite a lot about Four Square Development, Bill Trelawney, and his silent partner. I think that's why he's dead."

My heartbeat sped up. "Lorraine, are you telling me you know the identity of Four Square's fifth partner?"

"No. At first, I thought it was Bill Trelawney, but in an e-mail he had printed out, Tim called Bill small potatoes and insisted Bill introduce him to the fifth partner." She took a drink of her coffee.

"Tim thought he was working his way up through the ranks and that he would eventually work his way into one of the positions vacated by the members of Four Square Development who'd gone to prison."

"Why would he want that?" I asked. "He saw where it got the other four."

Lorraine closed her eyes. "I believe he thought lightning wouldn't strike in the same place twice." She opened her eyes and expelled a long, sad breath. "He'd tell me he was working on something that could make enough money to get us out of Tallulah Falls. I never really knew what it was, but I didn't ask, either. I didn't care." A tear trickled out the corner of her left eye. "I drove him to this with my materialistic attitude. I know I did."

"He was responsible for his own actions," I said, taking a drink of now-lukewarm coffee and remembering what Detective Nash had said about Lorraine's greed and how she'd browbeaten poor Timothy.

"What happened?" I asked. "Didn't he ever get what he considered enough money for the two of you to follow through with your plans?"

"No. Then he lost the store, and I left him." She reached for a napkin and dabbed at her eyes and nose. "I thought it would make him come to his senses and stop chasing whatever crazy scheme he was involved with."

I got up to get the coffeepot and topped off our cups. There wasn't a delicate way to ask Lorraine if she'd screwed up and the money had meant more to Timothy than she had, so I didn't say anything. Instead, I sat back down, poured milk into my coffee, and watched it turn a delicious shade of caramel.

"The day he died, he'd called me and said, 'By tonight, we'll have everything we'll ever need.' Then he said he'd be by to get me and . . . and he . . . he told me he loved me." She sobbed into the napkin. "I waited for him until the police came that next morning." She reached for another napkin.

"I'm sorry I blamed you. I needed to blame someone." Her shoulders shook as she buried her face in her hands.

"We have to find the person who's really at fault," I said. "We have to find the silent partner. None of us will be safe until we do."

CHAPTER SEVENTEEN

I sat up late that night, stitching and thinking. By the next morning, I'd finished my tote bag, and had brought it with me to share with the class that day. Now I was working on the first of Riley's baby bibs — the sleepy teddy bear. I figured it shouldn't take long to finish, and it was so adorable, it was a pleasure to watch it come together — sort of like a jigsaw puzzle. Plus, it was a welcome distraction.

After Lorraine had left the night before, I'd cleaned up the kitchen, let Angus inside, and tried to come up with a plot worthy of a television mystery.

Charlie's Angels would have me go to work as a teller with big hair in a short dress with a revealing neckline to determine whether or not the "silent partner" worked at the bank.

Columbo would have me wearing a trench coat and questioning the residents of Tallulah Falls with such inquiries as "Ah . . . Blake . . . I . . . ah . . ." I'd scratch my head. "I can't seem to recall. Where were you the night of the murda?"

Kojak would have me going from person to person, asking, "Who loves ya, baby?" while sucking on a lollipop. Plus, I'd be bald. I shuddered at the very idea.

Remington Steele would have me working side by side with Detective Nash, who'd suavely take all the credit while I did all the work.

Murder, She Wrote would have Todd demanding, "What business is it of yours that my name was in Bill Trelawney's ledger, Ms. Singer?"

By the end of the evening, I'd decided to turn this case over to *Psych, Monk,* or *The Dukes of Hazzard.* The first two because I love the shows, and those guys can figure anything out. And make you laugh while doing it. The third because, at this point, it would be such a welcome relief to blame everything on Boss Hogg and call it a day. The trouble was Boss Hogg was a buffoon, not a murderer.

Sadie came in after MacKenzies' Mochas' morning rush. Since some brain fog lingered from last night, I didn't think to conceal what I was doing until after Sadie had already seen that I was working on a bib.

Seeing the look in my eyes, she said, "Blake told you."

I figured I'd probably gotten Blake into enough trouble already, but then I reasoned it wasn't my fault his name was in Bill Trelawney's ledger. It took me so long to respond to Sadie's statement that I didn't have to.

"What did he tell you?" she asked.

"This is for Riley Kendall, actually," I said softly. "But Blake did tell me a little. Only that when you found out you had the flu, you were disappointed you weren't pregnant."

"I was disappointed," she said. "Now I'm thinking maybe it's for the best. Maybe Blake and I aren't ready to have a baby after all."

I didn't respond to that one. It wasn't for me to express an opinion on whether or not Blake and Sadie were ready to start a family.

She picked up the picture of the finished design I was stitching. "This is sweet." She set it back down. "What do you think?"

"Oh, I love it. I think it's as cute as can be." Whenever possible, go for the easy answer.

273

"You know I wasn't talking about the bib."

Unfortunately, it's not always possible to get away with the easy answer, especially with someone who knows you well. I sighed. "Only you and Blake can decide when you're ready to take that step." I should've quit while I was ahead, but I didn't. "Blake spoke as if you'd already made that decision."

"We had. But now he's raised all these trust issues. First, there was the ledger, and then he told you something he and I had agreed to keep between us."

"Maybe he thought you'd already told me or that you wouldn't care if I knew."

"That's beside the point, Marcy. I've always had the utmost trust in Blake, and now that trust has been shaken."

I silently went back to cross-stitching the bear.

"So how come you're making this for Riley?" Sadie asked.

"She commissioned it," I said. "She just learned she's pregnant with a girl, and she wants me to make some bibs and a blanket."

"I see. Well, good for her." She gave me a wry laugh. "You should start doing seminars: How to Make Your Enemies Your Bosom Buddies."

I smiled. "Maybe I should. Last night, I

had coffee with Lorraine Enright."

Sadie blinked. "You had coffee with Lorraine Enright? The same Lorraine Enright who barged into your home and threatened to file a wrongful-death suit against you?"

"That's the one. With all the sugar she put in her coffee, I doubt she ever went to sleep last night . . . even though the coffee was decaffeinated."

"Are you out of your mind?" she asked. "First you buddy up with Riley, and now Lorraine? Would you like to go down to the beach and throw chum in the water so we can draw more sharks in?"

I laughed. "That's a good one. Seriously, though, I need those women's help if I'm ever going to find out what really happened to Timothy Enright and Bill Trelawney. What's that old saying? 'Keep your friends close and your enemies closer.' "

"Just don't lose sight of who your enemies are. Neither one of those women is trustworthy. When Riley dumped Todd a few years ago for Keith Kendall, I knew she was a backstabber."

"Wait. If Todd and Riley were an item, then why had Todd and Norman Patrick never met before we visited Mr. Patrick at the prison?" I asked.

Sadie rolled her eyes. "Because Todd

275

wasn't good enough for Miss High-and-Mighty to introduce to her father, that's why. Todd was only a stepping-stone on Riley's path to Keith. And, believe me, she stomped all over him."

"Maybe so. But Todd told me he's known Riley for years, and, in fact, he couldn't say enough good things about her."

Sadie looked down at her folded hands.

My eyes widened. "He's still hung up on her! That's why you fixed the two of us up the night of my open house. I'm supposed to be Todd's rebound." I slammed the bib I was working on down onto the ottoman and stood up. "Thank you so very much, Sadie. I truly appreciate it."

"Look, it's not like that. Todd has dated since the breakup with Riley. After all, that was more than three years ago. But there haven't been any serious relationships." She shrugged. "Kind of like you and David."

I shook my head. "Don't even go there. I cannot believe you raked me over the coals for a little harmless flirting with Ted Nash after you fixed me up with someone who's still pining over another woman."

"He isn't pining," Sadie said. "He's over Riley. I just didn't want to see him get hurt again, that's all."

"You didn't want to see *him* get hurt?

That's precious. Thanks again."

"What? I don't want to see you get hurt, either."

"Why did you even want me to come here, Sadie?" I asked, my eyes filling with tears. "Why did you even bother?"

"I don't know," she answered, heading for the door. "Maybe it was a mistake."

"Maybe it was."

After Sadie left, I went to the bathroom to dry my eyes and repair my makeup. I heard the bell jingle and knew someone had come in. I wondered if Sadie had returned, so I waited a second to give her a chance to call out for me before I came back out into the shop. I needn't have wasted the thought. It wasn't Sadie. It was Vera, and she had already settled in on the navy sofa facing the window and begun stitching.

"Hello," she said, smiling at me. Her smile faded. "You've been crying."

"I'm fine."

"No, you aren't." She patted the sofa cushion. "Come sit here by me. Is it that identity-theft thing?"

"No." I sank onto the sofa beside her. "It's a fight-with-my-best-friend thing."

"You mean Sadie?"

I nodded. "We got into a huge argument, and I asked her why she even bothered getting me to move here, and she said it was a mistake." Fresh tears threatened, and I placed my index fingers beneath my eyes to dam them. I refused to give Sadie the satisfaction of making me redo my makeup a second time. Even if she didn't know it.

Vera clucked her tongue. "You know as well as I do your moving to Tallulah Falls was not a mistake."

"I wish I did know that."

"I believe deep down you do," Vera said. "As for you and Sadie, the two of you are enough like sisters that you probably fight and make up on a regular basis. Am I right?"

"We've fought a lot more since I moved here."

"Because you've seen each other more. You're like Lucy and Ethel. They fought and made up every other episode of *I Love Lucy.*"

I almost grinned at that.

"Tell you what. John is out of town this week for some sort of banking business. Let's you and I go out for a nice meal before class tonight. It will do us both a world of good."

I did smile at that. "You're on." I nodded toward her tote bag. "How are those half stitches coming?"

She held the tote up proudly. "You tell me."

"You're doing fantastic." And she was, too. I could now make out the entire teacup and part of the teapot.

Vera's cheerful attitude was contagious. I picked up Riley's teddy-bear bib, and Vera and I stitched and laughed and enjoyed the rest of the afternoon.

At closing time, I left to take Angus home. Vera and I decided to meet at the restaurant in half an hour. I'd no sooner parked the Jeep than my cell phone rang. It was Todd.

"Hey, are you busy tonight?" he asked.

"As a matter of fact, I am."

"That's right. You have class tonight, don't you?"

"Yes, I do."

"Would you like to grab a quick bite to eat before class, then?"

"I'm sorry, I can't," I said. "I have plans." I didn't elaborate. Let him think whatever he'd like.

"Well, then . . . I hope you have a good time," Todd said.

We ended the conversation, and I ranted to Angus the entire time I was feeding him and getting myself ready to go back out.

"Let him take some other rebound girl out to dinner," I said. "Besides, I didn't treat him like he did me when I asked about his name being in the ledger, did I, Angus? When he asked about dinner, I could've simply answered 'Nope' and left . . . I mean, hung up." I turned to get Angus' reaction. "Right?"

He slurped his tongue up the side of my face.

I smiled and kissed the top of his head. It was nice to know somebody loves me no matter what.

The restaurant was so dimly lit I had a difficult time finding Vera at first. Then she stood up, yelled "Yoo-hoo, Marcy!" and waved.

I grinned and refused to be embarrassed. I was here to have a good time. If Vera wanted to swing from the chandelier by her toenails, so be it. I might even be persuaded to join her.

That scenario became more likely than I'd dreamed when I arrived at the table and saw that Vera was three-quarters of the way through her second margarita.

The waitress came by for my drink order.

"Water, please," I said. "I'm the designated driver."

"Oh pooh," Vera said, flinging her wrist. "You really must try the margaritas. They're delightful."

I shook my head at the still-waiting waitress, and she went off to get my water.

"This place makes the best margaritas in the whole wide world," she said.

I tried to steer the discussion toward more sober ground. "Does John have to work out of town often?" I asked.

"Oh, sure. Once a month or so. It varies. Sometimes he's gone a day, and sometimes it's a week. You never know." She finished the margarita. "I should have another one of these."

"Why don't we wait until after we eat?" I asked. "It'll taste so much better then."

"You're right," she said. "It will." She grimaced. "I just remembered I forgot to each lunch today."

"Which is probably why those margaritas went straight to your head," I said with a smile.

"Better to go straight to the head than straight to the hips," she said.

The waitress returned with my water and took our orders. I requested the chicken Parmesan, and Vera ordered the same.

Once the waitress left, I asked Vera, "Do you and John have any children?"

"No." Her eyes welled up a little. "I can't."

"I'm so sorry." Mentally, I was kicking myself. Hard. Of course Vera had no children. If she did, she'd have talked about them.

"I'd have been a good mother," she said.

"I know you would have." I quickly scanned the restaurant for something else to talk about. I saw a red-haired woman seated a few tables away with her back to us. "Say, is that Lorraine Enright?"

Vera turned. She squinted back at me and then looked toward the redhead. "I think that *is* Lorraine."

The woman turned to look at something to her left, and I saw that it was indeed Lorraine Enright. She noticed us and quietly said something to her dining companion, an older male. Her father, maybe? He nodded in response to whatever Lorraine said and patted her hand. She grabbed her purse and left the restaurant, going the opposite way from where Vera and I were sitting.

After we ate, I convinced Vera to let me take her home. I told her she could call me tomorrow morning and I'd leave the shop long enough to bring her to retrieve her car.

Class went well. Everyone seemed to like the tote bag I'd made featuring Angus' face and embellished with dog-bone buttons. When Reggie wondered aloud where Vera could be, I mentioned we'd had dinner together but that Vera wasn't feeling well

282

afterward and I had taken her home.

When I got home, Lorraine Enright had left a strange message on my answering machine.

"I saw you and Vera Langhorne at the restaurant this evening. I'm sorry I left in such a rush. That guy I was with is a private investigator I hired to help me find out what happened to Tim and to our bank account. I didn't want anybody to see me talking with you. It could be dangerous. For both of us."

CHAPTER EIGHTEEN

I stopped by MacKenzies' Mochas before opening the shop the next morning. I'd overslept and hadn't had time to make coffee, and I desperately needed a latte.

"The usual?" Blake asked as I stepped up to the counter.

"Please."

"So . . . how was your date last night?"

"She was a barrel of laughs last night," I said, "but I doubt she'll be all that chipper this morning."

He gave me a lopsided grin. "She?"

"Vera Langhorne. John is out of town, so we had dinner together before class."

"Ah." He nodded and chuckled. "And here we were thinking you had a date with our resident Wyatt Earp. Todd mentioned you were busy, so we thought you might be out with Ted."

"We?" I asked coolly.

"Sadie, Todd, and I."

"Gee, thank you for letting me know why my ears were burning last night." I paid for my latte and strode to the door.

"Oh, hey, come on. It wasn't like that."

I ignored him.

I let Angus out of the Jeep and unlocked the shop. I went into the office to store my purse, tote, and jacket. When my cell phone rang, I sat down at my desk and answered it there.

"Marcy, it's Lorraine Enright. Are you alone?"

I looked at Angus, who was busy chasing his tennis ball around the office, and decided he probably wasn't listening. "Yes. Why do you ask?"

"I just can't risk us being overheard, that's all. I'm assuming you got the message I left on your machine last night."

"I got it," I said. "I didn't entirely understand it, but I got it."

"Things are getting weird. After I got home from your house the other night, someone called and asked me if I knew the identity of Four Square Development's silent partner."

"Let me guess — when you did a star-six-nine, the number the caller had used was unknown."

"What?" she asked. "No. I didn't even

think to check that. I was too scared."

"If it was the same person who called my house last week, it wouldn't have mattered."

"Then you've been getting calls, too?"

"Only the one night. Was this the first call you'd received?"

"Yes. Yesterday morning I phoned Riley to ask her about it. She told me about the baby and said she needs to be more careful now."

"More careful how?" I asked.

"She said she can't be involved with this investigation anymore, and she gave me the private detective's number."

I wondered if Mr. Patrick had warned his daughter away from Lorraine and me. True, Riley had been at the shop on Monday morning, but that was to commission embroidery projects for the baby.

"You mentioned in your message that the investigator is helping you determine what happened to your husband and to your bank account," I said. "What did you mean? Was there a freeze put on your account or something?"

"No, it's gone. The money is gone. A couple days after Timothy died, I went by the ATM and was told there were insufficient funds in my account. I stormed into the bank and went straight to John Langhorne's office."

I remembered Vera's version of that episode. So far, it was right on target with Lorraine's.

"When I told him to fix whatever problem there was with the account, he told me Timothy came in and closed the account the day he died."

"If your husband was planning on the two of you leaving town, I suppose that makes sense," I said. "Doesn't it?"

"That part does. But where did the money go? When the coroner gave me Timothy's effects, there was no money except for twenty dollars in his wallet." She expelled a long breath. "Fortunately, I've always kept a separate savings account, so I've been okay. But I need the rest of our money. And, honestly, I cannot imagine where that money went . . . unless whoever killed Timothy took it."

"I'm really sorry," I said, "about everything. Please keep me posted on whatever your investigator is able to find out."

"I will. And if you find out anything you think I should know, you've got my number."

It wasn't until after lunchtime that Vera called and asked me to take her to her car. I left Angus napping in the shop. Not everyone with a hangover can stomach warm dog breath panting in her face, and the mess that warm dog breath panting in her face could cause was one I shuddered to think about, much less clean up.

I was happy to see that Vera didn't appear to be much the worse for wear after all. Other than dark under-eye circles her concealer had been unable to hide, she looked fine.

"How do you feel?" I asked.

"Eh," she said, making a waffling hand gesture. "I'm a bit queasy and have a dull headache, but I'm pretty good. I plan on enjoying the rest of the day quietly, so it's no big deal."

"Good. Bet you won't be working on your teapot today, though."

She smiled. "No. Tiny stitches and an achy head aren't a wise combination. Have you and Sadie made up yet?"

"Not yet."

"Don't worry. You will."

Given my exchange with Blake this morning, I wasn't too sure about that.

Later, I was sitting at the counter, working on Riley's sleepy-teddy-bear bib. Angus was napping in his huge bed, and Jill was staring at the cash register, wondering why we hadn't had more customers today. Okay, just so you know, I'm only joking about Jill. I don't believe her to be real person or anything like that. . . . Although if she were, she'd have been staring at the cash register, wondering why we hadn't had more customers.

"I imagine it's the sunshine, Jill," I said. "People know winter is coming, and they'd better enjoy the nice weather while they can. Besides, it's the middle of the week. Who — besides us, and maybe Vera — thinks about beginning a new embroidery project in the middle of the week?"

So I talk to Jill once in a while. But in my defense, this whole Timothy Enright, Bill Trelawney, Four Square Development deal was driving me insane.

I decided to take stock of the facts I knew. Timothy Enright had come to my open house with the intention of telling me something. According to his estranged wife, he was coming to get her that night and they were leaving town. He'd closed out their joint bank account earlier that day. Either their account had dwindled down to twenty bucks — which wouldn't take them very far out of town, or somewhere between the bank and my shop, Mr. Enright had lost, been robbed of, or had spent their money.

He had then collapsed on my storeroom floor while trying to leave a message about Four Square's fifth partner. Why was the identity of Four Square Development's fifth partner so important to Timothy Enright that he was scratching it onto my wall with a tapestry needle and his last ounce of strength? The last piece of information I had about Timothy Enright was that his death had been ruled an accident due to alcohol poisoning.

Bill Trelawney had known Timothy Enright behaved badly at the open house, but he hadn't known Mr. Enright had been found dead in the storeroom the next morning. I still thought that one was odd. Mr. Trelawney had freaked when I'd mentioned the message Mr. Enright had scratched onto the wall, and it wasn't because he was concerned about the marred paint. Mr. Trelawney had been deeply involved with Four Square Development and was supposedly the only person — besides Timothy Enright — who knew the identity of Four Square Development's fifth partner. After reading the writing on the wall — literally — he hurried off and wound up shot in a remote area of town. He was shot with a .38-caliber pistol, and, apparently, I'm one of the few people in Tallulah Falls who doesn't own one of those.

Riley Kendall, who once broke Todd's heart into forty-eight-and-a-half pieces, hadn't liked me at all and had basically told me to mind my own business about Four Square Development when I first met her. Later that night, Sadie and I overheard Riley telling Lorraine Enright that she needed to find out what and how Timothy knew about Four Square.

And why was Riley running hot and cold with Lorraine? I took it that Lorraine had been her client for quite some time and that Timothy had been her father's client. I could fairly easily understand her fickle attitude toward me, although I did wonder if Mr. Patrick had told her — as she had reported to me — to give me another chance and try to help me out, or if he'd told her to keep an eye on me. After all, I'd said the adage to Sadie only yesterday: Keep your friends close and your enemies closer.

I put the final stitch in the sleepy bear, threaded a needle with a single black strand of embroidery floss to do the backstitching, and wondered how on earth it would all turn out.

The rest of the week was uneventful. Business was steady if a little slow, though I did sell a few big-ticket items, including an exquisite set of handmade Japanese embroidery needles. I taught the Wednesday and Thursday evening embroidery classes. I didn't hear from Riley, Lorraine, or Sadie. And I brought my coffee from home, so Sadie didn't hear from me, either. Nor did I hear from Todd or Detective Nash.

I did hear from Margaret Trelawney. She sounded sad. She told me she was calling to make sure I was doing all right, but there was more there. There was too much she wasn't saying. The entire call just didn't feel right to me, so I offered to come for a visit.

On Friday at around two o'clock, I closed the shop, took Angus home to play in the backyard, plugged Sylvia Shaw's address into my GPS, and headed for Portland. It was more than a two-hour drive from Tallulah Falls. Still, by my calculations, I'd get to Portland in time to avoid getting caught in rush hour traffic. I could visit with Mrs. Trelawney and Sylvia, make sure Mrs. Trelawney was okay, and be back here before it got late.

The closer I got to Portland, the heavier the traffic got. I guess there were lots of people getting a jump on the weekend. Also, the closer I got to Portland, the hungrier I got.

Not wanting to arrive at Sylvia's house with my stomach rumbling, I pulled in to a burger joint. I'd intended to use the drive-through window; but as I pulled around the side of the building, one of the customers sitting inside near a window caught my eye and sparked my curiosity. He looked so much like John Langhorne, it was scary. And he was sitting with a woman and two young men who lacked the appearance of fellow bankers.

I parked the Jeep. Overcome with curiosity that the man inside the restaurant could possibly be Mr. Langhorne, I snagged my Giants baseball cap from the backseat and kept my sunglasses on. I also took my wallet from my oversized yellow purse and placed the purse on the passenger's-side floor.

I went inside and walked to the counter. I looked straight ahead, as if I were merely a woman on a quest for a cheeseburger, which is what I actually had been before I saw the creepy John Langhorne look-alike.

I got my burger and soft drink and found a booth. Fortunately, there was one where I could sit with a row of plants to my left, so I was close enough to hear the group's conversation and yet remain unobserved.

". . . you have to leave tonight, John," the

woman was saying. "The weather is supposed to turn bad."

"That's why I'm leaving while the weather is on my side, sweetheart."

That voice gave me goose bumps. That man *was* John Langhorne.

"But don't worry, Mark," he continued. "I'll be here for your football game next Saturday."

"Cool," a young man's voice said.

"Hey, Dad," the other young man said, "while you're in Culver City, could you swing by that gourmet shop I love and get me a box of those hazelnut truffles?"

The man laughed. "Is it the truffles you love or that cute brunette who works the counter?"

"She is cute," the young man replied. "And it wouldn't hurt if you'd mention that I'm majoring in urban development. . . . You know, in case she likes men with potential and would maybe like to own her own gourmet shop one day."

"Or, if you think she prefers real men, Dad, invite her to come see me lead the Vikings to victory next Saturday."

"Oh yeah? And what would Jennifer say if she heard you talking like that? Let me think. 'Give me a D, give me a U, give me

an M and a P. What do they spell? Du—'
Ow!"

"Boys, stop that," the woman said. "Your
dad won't get to see you for a week. Let's
not send him off with the two of you quar-
reling."

"Aw, he's used to it, Mom. He knows
we're only fooling around."

"That's right, Emma," the man said.
"Boys will be boys."

That can't possibly be John Langhorne, I
told myself. *So what if he looks and sounds
uncannily like Vera's husband? He couldn't
possibly be, because that man is obviously
married to Emma and those young men are
their sons.*

I stood up and took my unwrapped burger
to the trash. This time I looked directly at
the family. And they looked at me. In fact,
one of the young men gave me quite a once-
over as I passed.

And there was no doubt in my mind that
his father was John Langhorne.

CHAPTER NINETEEN

I arrived at Sylvia's split-level home, feeling like a James Bond martini — shaken, not stirred. From the restaurant to Sylvia's house, I'd tried to envision a scenario that made even a modicum of sense.

The man was John Langhorne's identical twin. Their mother, unable to tell them apart, had called them both John. It had made her life so much easier. She could call, "John, come eat your dinner!" and both boys would race to the table.

Okay. That was stupid. But it gets worse. My other theories ran the gamut from clone to parallel universe. So, beyond trying to make myself believe that seeing a man who looked and sounded exactly like John Langhorne and whose first name was John was merely an extraordinary coincidence, all that was left was the knowledge that John Langhorne was leading a double life.

I parked in Sylvia's driveway and checked

my appearance in the visor mirror. The Giants cap had left my hair flat, and the shock of seeing John Langhorne with a wife who was not Vera — along with two sons — had left me pale. I remembered Vera's tortured expression when she'd told me she was unable to have children, as I dug through my purse for a lipstick. I found my favorite shade — a rosy mauve — but putting it on didn't do much to ameliorate my wan complexion.

I flipped the mirror back up, got out of the Jeep, and walked to Sylvia's door. Before I could raise my hand to ring the doorbell, Mrs. Trelawney flung open the door and enveloped me in a bear hug. She had surprising strength for a woman her age.

She then held me at arm's length so she could examine me. "You don't look well, dear. Are you feeling all right?"

"I'm just a little tired from the drive, I guess. How are you?"

"I'll do," she said. "Come on inside. Sylvia has made a tea for the three of us."

I thought Mrs. Trelawney had misspoken when she'd said *a tea* until I saw that Sylvia had, in fact, prepared much more than a pot of tea. On the dining room table, there were blueberry scones, oatmeal-raisin cookies, two fruit platters, and apple-walnut muffins. Although my appetite had deserted me at the restaurant, it now returned with a vengeance.

Sylvia came from the kitchen with a tea tray. "We were beginning to think you'd gotten lost." She placed the tea tray on the table.

"Sorry." I shrugged. "Friday traffic."

"Hmm. You and Maggie have a seat and tell me which type of tea you'd like. I have orange pekoe, green, white, and chamomile."

I chose green, Mrs. Trelawney opted for orange pekoe, and Sylvia made herself a cup of chamomile.

As we filled our plates with Sylvia's goodies, Mrs. Trelawney asked me if everything appeared to be getting back to normal in Tallulah Falls. I knew she was asking because she wanted to come home. While I couldn't blame her for that, I still didn't feel it was safe for her to come back home. I wanted to stress that to both Mrs. Trelawney and Sylvia, but I didn't want to scare them.

"Riley Kendall is pregnant," I said to buy myself some time. "She came in and commissioned me to make some things for the baby."

"Oh, how nice," Mrs. Trelawney said.

"That's not what she meant about things getting back to normal," Sylvia said. "She's asking if there are any new developments in the case and whether or not you think it's safe for her to come home."

So much for tact and trying to candy-coat my concerns. "No," I said. "I don't think it's safe for Mrs. Trelawney to come home yet." I looked at Mrs. Trelawney. "The night after your house was broken into, I got an anonymous call from someone asking me what you know."

Sylvia returned the scone she'd been holding to her plate and wiped the corners of her mouth with her napkin before answering. "I saw a man skulking about outside the house that night after the break-in. I know this will sound strange, but for some reason, he reminded me of that young man who runs the coffee shop."

"MacKenzies' Mochas?" I asked.

"Yes. That's the one."

"Did you call the police?" I asked.

"Of course. But by that time, the man was gone."

"Did you tell the police who you suspected?" I asked.

Mrs. Trelawney watched our back-and-forth exchange as if she were at a tennis match.

"Yes," Sylvia said. "They found him at some place called the Brew Crew. He said he'd been there during the time of the incident, and the proprietor confirmed it." She picked up her scone. "I must have been mistaken, but he did resemble that young man very much." She shook her head and took a bite of the scone.

I digested this information while eating a strawberry. Based on the phone call I'd received from Blake the night after the Trelawney break-in, I wondered if he had been the man Sylvia saw . . . and if Todd had lied to protect him. That both Sylvia and I would see dead ringers for Tallulah Falls residents was too much of a coincidence for at least one of us not to have seen who we think we saw. See?

"How much do either of you know about John Langhorne?" I asked.

"I don't know the man at all," Sylvia said. "I met him at Bill's visitation, but he didn't leave me with much of an impression."

"I know he travels a lot," Mrs. Trelawney said.

I nodded. "I think I saw him here in Portland. He was with a woman and two college-age boys. They called him Dad."

Mrs. Trelawney frowned. "That's peculiar. I never knew John had been married

300

before Vera."

I smiled. It was the one scenario that hadn't even crossed my overly dramatic mind. The woman was John's first wife, and they'd maintained an amicable relationship for the sake of their children.

"Here I was thinking Mr. Langhorne was leading some sort of double life," I said with a laugh. "I get it from my mother. She's a costume designer."

"In Hollywood?" Sylvia asked.

"Yes. Although right now, she's on location in New York."

"Does she know Sean Connery?" Sylvia asked. "I think he's marvelous."

"How about Bob Hope?" Mrs. Trelawney asked.

"He's dead," Sylvia said.

"Jack Parr?" Mrs. Trelawney asked.

"Dead."

"George Burns?"

"Dead," Sylvia said. "They're all dead."

To end the Hollywood obituary, I said, "I'll speak with Chief Myers to see if he has any new developments in the case." I patted Mrs. Trelawney's arm. "I know everyone in Tallulah Falls wants you to come home as soon as possible."

"And God knows I want that, too," Sylvia muttered.

■ ■ ■ ■

When I got home, everyone and his mother — actually, it was everyone and *my* mother — had left a message on my answering machine, wondering where I was. I always turn off my cell phone when I'm driving. Otherwise, it's too much of a distraction for me.

Besides Mom, there were messages from Sadie, Todd, Ted Nash, and Reggie. I called Mom first. I didn't think there would be any surprises coming from her.

"How are you, love?" she asked. "It appears I'll be wrapping up here in a couple weeks. Maybe then I can pay you a visit."

"That would be terrific. I'd love to have you pay us a visit, and I know Angus would eat it up." Literally. Mom is constantly giving him little treats when she's around.

"What else is going on in your little world?" she asked.

"Sadie and I had an argument."

"Don't tell me she's borrowing your jewelry without asking," Mom said with a giggle. "That's what the two of you were always fighting about in college."

"I know, and it still bugs me that she did that. It only goes to show how inconsiderate she is."

"Whoa, now. I didn't intend to bring up past indiscretions. What's going on between the two of you?"

"She set me up with a guy even though she thinks he's still pining over his old girlfriend."

"How old?" Mom asked. "Are we talking days, weeks, months, or years?"

"Three years."

"Has he mentioned this woman to you?"

"Only when I brought up her name. At that point, I didn't know they'd ever dated."

"Ah," Mom said. "And what did he say about her?"

"Um . . . I think he told me she was fair."

"Fair as in *beautiful,* or fair as in *just?*"

I laughed. "Just, Mom. Who describes pretty women as *fair* anymore?"

"You'd be surprised. Did he tell you they'd dated?"

"No."

"Did he go on and on about how great she is?"

"No."

"Did he say something along the lines of, 'She's a selfish hag, but I have to admit she's fair'?"

"No, Mom, he didn't say anything like

303

that. All he said was that she was tough but fair."

"Then he's over her."

"Are you sure?" I asked.

"Positive. What I'm not sure about is whether you're still pining for David."

"I'm not, Mom. I'm completely over him. . . . You haven't seen him or anything lately, have you?"

"No. Have you heard from him?"

"No. I wonder if he even knows I've moved."

"He knows. Too many of your friends know for him not to be aware of it. Are you sure you're okay?"

"Absolutely. Hurry and wrap that shoot up, will you?"

"As quickly as I can, love. As quickly as I can."

After talking with Mom, I felt better about talking with everyone else . . . except maybe Reggie and Detective Nash. I could never be sure of why those two might be calling. And Todd. I wasn't really ready to talk with him, either. He might be over Riley, but I had to wonder if he was helping Blake cover up something about Four Square Development . . . or vice versa.

So, in reality, the only other person I felt halfway ready to talk with was Sadie. I dialed her number and was greeted with, "Marce, where have you been? I've been worried sick."

"I went to Portland to visit Mrs. Trelawney. What's the big deal?"

"The big deal is that I came to see you at three thirty this afternoon and saw that you'd closed the shop. I thought maybe you'd caught my stomach bug and gone home. When I called and couldn't reach you at home, Blake and Todd went out looking for you."

"Even if you guys thought I had a stomach bug, wouldn't it make sense that I might've gone to the doctor?" I asked. "I mean, I am a grown woman."

"I know that, Marcy. But with all the crazy stuff that's been going on, I was worried. Excuse me."

"I'm sorry. You're right. It's just that we hadn't spoken since Tuesday, and I . . . I didn't think to leave word with anyone that I'd gone to Portland."

"How is Mrs. Trelawney?" Sadie asked.

"She's all right. She and Sylvia are driving each other bonkers."

"Did she say when she'd be coming home?"

"No. She and Sylvia asked whether or not it was safe for her to come home, and I said

I didn't think it was yet."

"You don't?" Sadie asked. "Why not?"

"I think there's someone still out there who believes Mrs. Trelawney knows too much about Four Square Development. And it's like Ted Nash once told me: This person has already killed to protect his secret twice — well, once if you believe Timothy Enright's death was an accident. Oh, and hey, guess what?"

"What?"

I told her about seeing John Langhorne in the burger restaurant in Portland and how I'd tried in vain to put it all together until Mrs. Trelawney said she hadn't realized John had a first wife. We had a good laugh over that.

"I thought he was doing well to get Vera," Sadie said. "Much less anyone else. What did this first wife look like?"

"She was really attractive. And the boys were good-looking, too."

"Hmm. Maybe Mr. Langhorne was handsome when he was young," Sadie said. "Before the pressures of banking got to him."

"Yeah. Maybe."

We both dissolved into another laughing fit. It was good to have things back to normal between Sadie and me. I hate it

306

when we fight.

After speaking with Sadie, I felt like working on the MacKenzies' Mochas logo project I'd neglected while she and I were on the outs. I decided to turn in early, work on the project while propped up against the headboard of my bed, and talk with everyone else tomorrow. Stitching and listening to a calming playlist on my MP3 player was sure to relax me and ensure a good night's rest.

CHAPTER TWENTY

I was overly tired Saturday night and fell asleep before ten p.m. while sitting on the sofa in front of the television. I was watching a detective show; but I fell asleep so quickly, I never even really got the gist of what it was about.

I woke up about eleven o'clock. The detective show had gone off, but a true-crime show was running. I couldn't quite break through my lethargy long enough to get up and drag myself to bed, so I watched the show.

An elderly woman had killed her husband by giving him alcohol sponge baths to reduce his fever. The show was trying to determine whether his death had been accidental or intentional.

A coroner came on screen. "Doctors once prescribed these sponge baths for patients to reduce fever. However, it was discovered that isopropyl — or rubbing alcohol —

absorbs through the skin and suppresses the central nervous system."

A narrator explained that isopropyl is twice as deadly as ethyl alcohol, the alcohol found in alcoholic beverages, while a couple reenacted the sponge bath.

The show returned to the coroner. "An overdose of isopropyl can cause hemorrhaging in the trachea and bronchial tubes," he said gravely. "And our victim's autopsy showed that to be the case in his death."

I retrieved my wallet and took out Ted Nash's business card. He'd written his home number on the back. I snatched up the cordless phone and dialed the home number.

"Nash," he said.

"Ted, it's Marcy."

"Is everything okay?"

"I don't know. I've . . . I'm seeing something on television about isopropyl, and I'm wondering whether Timothy Enright's autopsy report showed signs of hemorrhaging in the trachea or bronchial tubes."

"I don't remember. But I'll look first thing in the morning and see," he said. "Are you sure everything is all right?"

"Yeah. I just . . . I don't know. I have a weird feeling. I'm probably wrong, but . . . check that out, would you?"

"I will. And I'll call or drop by and let you know as soon as I find out."

"Thanks," I said.

"You want to share this theory?" he asked.

"Not yet. It's too far-fetched." I laughed softly. "I'm really good at far-fetched."

"Sometimes far-fetched isn't."

"Tomorrow," I said. "After you find out what the autopsy report says, we'll talk about it."

"You got it. Get some sleep."

That would be easier said than done. The true-crime show had me thinking about how someone could have made Timothy Enright inhale, ingest, or absorb enough isopropyl through his skin to kill him.

After talking with Detective Nash, I went upstairs and changed into my pajamas. Angus stayed downstairs for the time being, but I knew he'd be up after the living room got cooler from the gas logs being turned off.

I lay in bed and thought about Timothy Enright. Who would want him dead? Four Square Development's fifth partner would. Lorraine was a possibility, if she was lying about the fact that her husband was trying to make enough money for the two of them to start anew somewhere else. By all accounts, Timothy cared deeply for his wife;

but arguably, he could've become tired of her manipulations.

Since that's all I knew about Mr. Enright, I turned my attention to Mr. Trelawney. Who would want the poor old landlord dead?

Once again, by all accounts, Bill Trelawney had been heavily involved with Four Square Development. But Mr. Trelawney had escaped discovery during the audit that put the other four principals in prison. Why hadn't they ratted him out?

It was shortly after coming to the shop and looking at the message Timothy Enright had etched into the wall that Mr. Trelawney was found shot to death in his car. Had that been a coincidence, or had he hurried to alert Four Square Development's fifth partner, who had also previously escaped detection?

If the fifth partner had killed Bill Trelawney, then what was his motivation? Mr. Trelawney had apparently been the only person entrusted with the fifth partner's identity, so why turn on him now? Was it that Mr. Trelawney realized the fifth partner had killed Timothy Enright? Maybe Mr. Trelawney was willing to put up with real estate fraud, but not murder.

I couldn't think of anyone else who might

want Mr. Trelawney dead. A crazed renter with a leaky faucet? But even that was a stretch.

Still, I'd been stretching my imagination like crazy lately. After seeing Mr. Langhorne in Portland, I'd deduced he was living a double life rather than that he'd been in a previous marriage. And, in my mind, I was accusing Blake of making frightening phone calls to me and breaking into the Trelawney house. There's no way Blake would do that. Would he? I mean, he readily admitted to Manu that he'd allowed Mr. Trelawney to use his financial information, and he hadn't gotten into trouble. Everything was fine. Whatever Blake did in the past was in the past.

I needed some sleep. Like Scarlett O'Hara, I'd think about it tomorrow.

I was dreaming I was in a classroom. I was getting ready to take a test when the bell started ringing. In fact, the bell was getting on my nerves, badly. I was searching for a way to turn it off when I awoke and realized it wasn't a school bell but the telephone ringing.

I clumsily took the phone out of its holder and pressed the Talk button. "Hello."

"Marcy? Marcy, it's Vera Langhorne.

Something terrible has happened. John has been in a car accident." She was sobbing.

"Calm down," I said, pushing myself up in bed. "How bad is it?"

"The California Highway Patrol told me he's in intensive care. I'm going to the hospital now. I wanted someone to know."

"Is someone driving you?"

"N-no. I'll make it all right."

I thought it was odd that it was me she reached out to, but she really seemed in desperate need of help. "Let me get up and get dressed, and I'll be right over," I said. "I can drive you to California."

"Really? Are . . . are you sure?"

"Positive. You're in no condition to drive."

"Thank you, dear."

I set the phone back in its charger and threw back the covers. Angus groaned.

"Me, too, buddy. I was hoping to sleep in. But this is important, and Vera would do the same for me."

I schlepped to the shower and quickly bathed and washed my hair. I dried my hair as soon as I got out of the shower and returned to the bedroom to throw on a blue track suit with a white V-neck T-shirt underneath. I had a long drive ahead of me, and I decided I might as well be comfortable.

I hurried downstairs, fed Angus, and let

him out into the backyard. The sky was still dark, partly because it was early and partly because there was a major storm heading our way.

I sighed, grabbed a granola bar, and headed for Vera's house. Before backing out of the driveway, I called MacKenzies' Mochas and left a voice-mail message.

"Hi, it's Marcy. It was too early to call you guys at home, but I'm taking Vera Langhorne to California. The highway patrol called and told her John has been in an accident. Anyway, would you please check on Angus? He's in the backyard, and it looks like it's going to storm. He hates storms. I'll call you back when I know more about Mr. Langhorne. Thanks!"

I dropped the phone into my purse and drove to the Langhornes' house. The porch light was on, but otherwise, the entire neighborhood was dark. I envied those people still asleep, and immediately felt guilty for the thought.

I parked in the driveway beside Vera's BMW. As I walked to the door, I thought about how strange this all felt. Tallulah Falls seemed like such a close-knit community. And yet the newest person in town was the one who two people had both turned to. Why was that? I understood that neither

Vera nor Mrs. Trelawney had children, but one would think they'd lived in Tallulah Falls long enough to have made friends closer than me. Was it that Tallulah Falls wasn't such a close-knit community after all? Had the recent criminal activity caused the people to shut themselves off from one another and become afraid to trust?

I rang the doorbell. Vera opened the door so quickly, I wondered if she'd been standing there waiting on me since she had first called.

"Come in quickly," she said, moving aside just enough to allow me entrance.

I noticed she was trembling. "Vera, it'll be okay."

She shut the door and turned off the porch light before turning back to me with wide, frightened eyes. "No, it won't."

John Langhorne stepped from the hallway into the room. He was holding a gun. I had a sick feeling it was a .38 caliber . . . probably the same one used to kill Bill Trelawney.

"What's going on?" I asked.

"Marcy," Mr. Langhorne said, shaking his head. "It wasn't bad enough for you to poke your nose into my business dealings, but then you had to follow me to Portland."

"I didn't follow you anywhere," I said. "I

went to Portland to visit Margaret Trelawney."

"Still, it was bad luck for you to run into me, Emma, and the boys. When I got home, Vera said she hadn't talked with you, but I knew it would be only a matter of time."

So my worst suspicions were true — it wasn't my overactive imagination. But I tried to play the innocent. "So what if you were having lunch with your ex-wife and sons," I said. "That's no big deal. Right?"

"She's my current wife," Mr. Langhorne said.

I looked at Vera, who had tears rolling down her face. She'd had a rough night.

"Whatever it is you plan to do," I said, "leave Vera out of it. You've put her through enough."

"How very noble. But she's already into it. Too late to leave her out now." He shook his head again. "I gave you every opportunity to be left out of it, as well, but you just kept on stirring up hornets' nests."

"Look," I said. "I don't know what you're talking about. I don't know anything about your business life or your personal life. I just want to take Vera with me and go home."

"Please, John," Vera said. "Just let us leave. We'll never tell anyone anything, and I'll never ask anything of you."

"And what will the fine residents of Tallu-lah Falls say when they see that we've separated, Vera? They'll say, 'Why did you two split up? You had such a wonderful marriage. You'd been together for so long.' And you won't be able to lie."

"I will. I will, John. I swear."

"I'll help her," I said. "We'll say the two of you simply grew apart. You could leave here and go to your family in Portland."

"Why would I do that?" he asked. "They'd drive me insane if I had to live with them all the time."

Too late, I thought.

"Then start somewhere fresh," I said.

"I can't do that, Marcy. My life is here. I've built up a successful business in Tallu-lah Falls. I'm on the city council. I'm important in this community. A man simply doesn't throw all that away on a whim." He waved the gun. "Let's go."

"Where are we going?" I asked.

"California. You're taking Vera to a hospital there, remember?"

I frowned and looked at Vera. She shook her head wearily.

"I don't understand. I —"

"Just go. You're driving. We're all going to hurry outside and get into your vehicle.

Vera, make sure there's no one out there."

Vera opened the door and peered outside. "I don't see anyone."

"Are you sure?"

"Positive."

"Good," he said. "Go."

We went out and got into the Jeep. I got in the driver's side, Vera sat on the passenger's side, and John got into the backseat, where he could continue threatening us with the gun.

"This is ridiculous," I said. "No one will believe I took Vera to a hospital in California because you were in an accident if you were never in an accident in California."

"Of course they will. My wallet was stolen, and the thief was the man in the car accident. Unfortunately, on your way to see about me, you and Vera had fatal accident yourself. It's tragic; it's poignant. All the neighbors will bring wonderful food, and I'll grieve my heart out." He looked all around. "Drive slowly, Marcy. I don't want you raising the suspicions of anyone who might be about. Although, I suppose it's reasonable that you'd be driving too fast . . . just as long as you don't get stopped by law enforcement."

I glanced at Vera from the corner of my eye. "Are you all right?"

"Not really." Her voice broke, and she rested her head against the glass.

"You know," Mr. Langhorne said, "I really will grieve over you, Vera. No man could've asked for a better wife."

Vera closed her eyes.

I drove slowly down the street where the Seven-Year Stitch was dark and abandoned. *Good-bye, Jill,* I thought. I almost cried in a fit of self-pity at that point, but I refused to believe this was it for me, that I was going to die at the hands of some psychopathic old man.

We met Blake's van. He was coming in to work early. I was glad. That meant he'd get my message and go check on Angus when he had time.

"Why Mr. Trelawney?" I asked.

"Excuse me?" Mr. Langhorne asked politely.

How strange was that? He was holding a gun on me and had already planned my demise, but he refused to be rude about it.

"Why did you kill them?"

"Oh, well, Tim was a blackmailer, and Bill had a real problem with Tim's death. I didn't think he could live without telling someone what I'd done. I couldn't risk that. Did he ever tell Margaret about my involvement with Four Square Development?"

"No. She told me she had no idea who the fifth partner was."

"Well, that's good. It'll save me an unpleasant task in Portland next week. Mark has a football game, you know."

"Oh yeah," I said. "Wish him luck for me." I slammed on the brakes. "Let's just stop this. We can work this out."

Mr. Langhorne cocked the gun. "Drive, Marcy. Or else I'll have to kill you and then wreck the Jeep myself. Take this time to pray or something. It'll make you feel better."

Taking that gun and beating you over the head with it would make me feel better.

I resumed driving. It was all I could do until I figured a way out of this.

CHAPTER TWENTY-ONE

"Can I ask you a question?" I asked Mr. Langhorne. "I mean, it's a long way to California. We might as well chat."

"Sure. Ask whatever you'd like."

"What happened to the money Timothy Enright took out of his account?"

He laughed. "He never took any money out of the account. He intended to, but there was no money to take."

"How could there be no money to take?" I asked. "Lorraine said Timothy was going to close out the account. How could he do that if there was no money?" I looked at Mr. Langhorne in the rearview mirror. He chuckled and shook his head as if I were a simpleton.

"When he entered the bank that afternoon," Mr. Langhorne said, "there was money in the account. He told me his plans, and I invited him to have a cup of my Café Cubano. Have you ever tried

Café Cubano?"

"No. What's that?"

"It's Cuban coffee. Very strong. It's not a sipping coffee. You shoot it, like tequila. And it will disguise the taste of anything."

"Like rubbing alcohol," I said.

"You're quite bright, Marcy. I think under different circumstances, you and I would have been great friends."

"Oh, sure," I said. "So, what were Timothy Enright's plans?"

"He wanted to get out while he was ahead, withdraw his money, leave town, yadda, yadda. Like you and Vera, he promised to take all his information to his grave . . . which he did. I mean, he tried not to, but in the end, he did."

"Why don't you trust anyone?" I asked. Yeah, I know it was a stupid question, but I was still trying to talk him into not killing Vera and me. "How do you know Mr. Enright wouldn't have kept his word?"

"It's hard to keep secrets. I know. They eat away at you. Besides, he'd grown a conscience. He'd seen Bill's ledger and knew we were taking advantage of . . . well, of people like you. He didn't think that was right. Especially when so many others were willing to give their consent."

"Like Blake."

"Sure. Blake didn't care what Bill did with his information as long as his debt was wiped out and he didn't get into any trouble. That one was a win-win."

"Then why did you start duping Bill's renters?"

"Once again, people have a hard time keeping secrets," he said. "If people don't know they're being used, they don't whine about it."

"So, why didn't Mr. Enright go to the authorities as soon as you told him there was no money in his account?" I asked.

"Because I told him I'd moved the money to another bank and wouldn't have it until the next day. Now stop talking. You're tiring me."

"Sorry."

We drove in silence for a few miles. I hoped Mr. Langhorne would doze off or something. But he kept sitting there in the middle of the backseat, holding the gun, as unwavering as a statue. If he'd only put the gun down at his side, maybe I could open the door and roll out onto the pavement. It would leave Vera in the lurch, but maybe Mr. Langhorne would be too busy trying to control the vehicle to hurt her. And maybe she'd take my cue and jump out also. Self-preservation is a powerful motivator.

"Up here," Mr. Langhorne said. "You need to get onto the 101."

Great. We were starting onto the highway. If I couldn't get Mr. Langhorne distracted on the secondary roads, how could I hope to catch a break on the highway? On the other hand, maybe a truck driver would glance down into the Jeep, notice a man with a pistol in my backseat, and alert the highway patrol.

"I'm too warm," I said, feigning a yawn. "It's making me sleepy."

"Then turn the heat off or put on the air conditioner," Mr. Langhorne said.

"Couldn't we stop up here at the side of the road and stretch our legs before getting onto the highway?" I asked.

"Needing to stretch your legs is the least of your worries. Keep driving."

I pulled onto the entrance ramp of the highway. "So, what's the plan, Mr. Langhorne? You're going to make us drive all the way to California to stage a car accident? Wouldn't it be easier to stage the accident here?"

Vera shook her head vehemently.

"You'd be found too quickly. Besides, I want it to appear realistic."

"How will you get back home?" I asked.

"In a rental car."

"But how —"

"Once again, you are making me weary with your chatter. Shut up and drive."

I had to figure out how to get away from this maniac. I looked at Vera. She was obviously terrified. I wondered if up until now she'd had any clue what Mr. Langhorne was capable of. Had she suspected his trips weren't strictly business?

As I merged into traffic, I cut off the car behind me. The driver blew the horn. I slammed on my brakes, and the driver of the other car had to swerve onto the left side of the road to avoid hitting me.

Mr. Langhorne hit me with the butt of the gun. "Stop driving like a lunatic. Are you trying to drag some innocent person into this?"

I wanted to scream that Vera and I were innocent and he'd dragged us into it, but my head was hurting and I didn't want another blow from the gun barrel. I didn't want to be shot, either. I decided to drive normally for a little while and maybe it would lull Mr. Langhorne into thinking I'd resigned myself to my fate.

We'd been driving on the highway for about fifteen minutes when Vera snapped out of her funk.

"Marcy, do you have a tissue in your glove

box?" she asked.

"I believe so. If not a tissue, I'm pretty sure there are some restaurant napkins in there," I said.

"Thank you." She put her hand on my arm and squeezed. "You're very kind." Her eyes bore into mine.

That squeeze meant something. She was getting ready to do something, and she wanted me to follow her lead.

She opened the glove compartment. Instead of a tissue, she took out my travel hair spray bottle. She whirled around in the seat and sprayed her husband in the eyes. I turned the Jeep toward the guardrail and slammed on the brakes.

Mr. Langhorne lurched forward. His eyes were watering, and I don't think he could see well. I grabbed his wrist and beat his bony hand against the console until I was able to take the gun.

"Run, Vera!" I shouted.

I unbuckled my seat belt and flung open the door. Vera was a little slower than I was, and Mr. Langhorne grabbed her by the arm. I opened the backseat and hit him with the butt of the pistol until he let her go. I owed him that one.

Vera and I began running back down the highway. We'd just passed an exit; and we knew if we could get to a gas station or somewhere else safe, we could call the police and be home free. Naturally, we'd left our purses and our cell phones behind in the Jeep as we'd made our escape.

I heard the Jeep roar back to life. I looked over my shoulder. "No way."

Mr. Langhorne plowed through the median and was racing down the other side of the highway. What was he doing? Was he going to get off at the exit and come back after us? Even if he did, I had the gun. What did he hope to do? Run us over with the Jeep?

Turns out, that was exactly what he hoped to do. When he got down below us, he ran through the median again and came after us.

I looked at Vera.

"Do it," she said.

"But I don't want to —"

"I'll do it." She jerked the gun out of my hand and began firing. She emptied the pistol into the windshield of the Jeep. She was a surprisingly good shot.

As the Jeep started to crash for the second time, I grabbed Vera and dove into a ditch on the other side of the guardrail. The Jeep crashed a few feet away from us, the horn blowing in one long, monotonous groan.

■ ■ ■ ■

A couple of people — a skinny black truck driver and a heavyset Caucasian cowboy in a pickup truck — saw what happened and stopped and asked whether they could help. Though there was a lot of rubbernecking, no one else was brave enough to stop . . . which was understandable, considering John had tried to kill us with the Jeep and Vera had emptied the contents of the pistol into the windshield.

Neither Vera nor I had the courage to go look into the Jeep to see what condition John was in. The cowboy went. He came back, looked at me, and shook his head.

I tried to explain the situation to the cowboy and the trucker, but everything came out in a jumbled mess. The trucker put a blanket around Vera's and my shoulders and told us everything would be fine.

A blue Oregon State Trooper's patrol car drove up. The officer got out of the car, assessed the situation, and radioed for paramedics and backup. That's when I realized Vera was still holding the gun limply at her side.

"Drop that," I told her as the officer drew his gun. "It's okay. She wouldn't shoot you.

She was using it only to defend herself . . . and me."

"Put your hands where I can see them," the officer said. "Both of you."

We held up our hands. The trucker and the cowboy backed slowly toward the officer. They put their hands up, too.

"What's going on here?" the officer asked.

The cowboy and the trucker started talking at once, telling the officer what they'd seen. Vera and I kept quiet.

And then, like John Wayne riding in to save the day — albeit an Indian John Wayne, which is, in a way, the epitome of irony — Manu Singh of the Tallulah Falls Police Department pulled up in his bronze-colored Bronco. I don't know when I'd ever been happier to see anyone. And when he spoke, I don't know when I'd ever heard sweeter words.

"You can put your gun away, Officer. I know these women."

CHAPTER TWENTY-TWO

After the paramedics had left with a deceased John Langhorne, and the tow truck had left with a deceased Jeep, the officer put Vera into his patrol car. I rode in the backseat of another officer's car — which was not a pleasant experience, but it was, like, fourth on my list of unpleasant experiences so far that day and it wasn't even nine a.m. yet. Manu followed us to the police headquarters.

The officers had already spoken with the truck driver, the cowboy, and Manu. They'd spoken briefly with Vera and me, too, but they had to "take us downtown" to talk with us a great deal more and to make everything official. Since it was determined that Vera had acted in self-defense, no charges were filed against her.

The gun was turned over to Manu as evidence after Manu told the officers at the scene that he believed ballistics tests would prove John Langhorne had used the gun to kill Bill Trelawney. I volunteered the information that Mr. Langhorne had confessed to killing both Mr. Trelawney and Mr. Enright, and that he had intended to murder Vera and me and make it look as if we'd died in a car accident. I told Manu how Mr. Trelawney had murdered Mr. Enright by putting rubbing alcohol in a cup of Café Cubano.

"But how did you know where to find us?" I asked Manu.

"Blake MacKenzie called me," Manu said. "He said you'd left a message on his answering machine, telling him and Sadie you were taking Vera Langhorne to California because her husband had been in a car accident and was in the hospital there. Then he explained that he'd seen you and Vera drive by in your Jeep and that there was a man in the backseat. Blake thought the man looked like John."

Manu had agreed with Blake that the situation was suspicious.

"I called the California Highway Patrol and confirmed that they had no record of any of their officers calling a Vera Langhorne of Tallulah Falls, Oregon, and reporting that her husband had been in an accident. That's when I got in my Bronco and tracked you using the GPS signal from your phone."

After all the Oregon State Police paperwork had been completed, the officers turned us over to Manu, who said he'd take us home. Manu warned Vera that an insurance investigator would be looking at the events surrounding John's death prior to paying out any benefits. She surprised us both by saying that was fine with her. She had her own accounts, which had been provided for her by her parents when she'd married, on the condition that they remain in her name only.

"They were filthy rich," Vera said. "Mother still is. Dad died in 'ninety-two. I guess the money is probably why John married me in the first place. My dad got John his job at the bank. We were members of the country club. Everyone thought highly of the Breck family." Her voice trailed off.

"I never knew your parents," Manu said. "I suppose they were before my time."

"They were before everyone's time," she said. "They left Tallulah Falls about forty years ago." She sighed. "Now what? What do I do with the rest of my life?"

"Now you go on," I said. "You go on and have a terrific life."

"I guess you're right. What other choice

do I have?"

That was more than two months ago. Both Halloween and Thanksgiving came and went, and we were heading into December. Mom has visited twice and said my adventure would make a fantastic movie. She's planning to put the word out among various producers and directors. She thinks Ron Howard could "do it up right."

I got a new red Jeep. It's exactly like the old one, only it's shiny and not smashed up. I don't think Angus has noticed the difference, but, of course, he never saw the Jeep when it was smashed up. I'm grateful for that. Who knows how that might have affected him?

Mrs. Trelawney has returned home, but Sylvia still comes to visit fairly often. They seem to have reached a new level of . . . let's call it tolerance. I wouldn't call them friends, but they seem to have a certain responsibility and grudging affection toward each other, for Mr. Trelawney's sake.

I still think Mr. Trelawney was a nice old man. I don't think he meant anybody any real harm. I believe he merely got caught up in John Langhorne's scheme and either enjoyed the money or the thrill of the game. I never found out how he knew Mr. Enright had been disruptive at the open house but didn't know he'd died in the storeroom. I also never found out why he suspected John Langhorne of killing Mr. Enright or why he went to confront him. Some secrets die with their keepers.

Manu, Reggie, and I discussed it over dinner one evening.

"I believe Tim Enright found out about John Langhorne from Bill Trelawney," Manu said. "I think it was accidental on Bill's part. But once the horse was out of the barn, there was no getting him back in."

"And I think John brought Timothy into the fold because his other coconspirators had been arrested," Reggie said. "He needed some new blood to liven up his operation."

"But why did Mr. Enright come to the open house looking for me?" I asked.

"He must've known Mr. Trelawney had stolen your identity and wanted to warn you," Manu said. "After searching John's offices at the bank and at home, here's what I was able to piece together. John, Bill, and Timothy had put their heads together in a new real estate fraud scheme."

"Lorraine told me she and her husband had fought about his working relationship with Bill Trelawney, and that's why she left him," I said.

"Which is why Tim wanted out," Manu said. "He went to John, intending to close out his and Lorraine's joint accounts so the two of them could leave town."

"He didn't want to wind up like the former Four Square Development partners, rotting away in prison while his wife moved on with her life," Reggie said.

"But when he tried to close out the account," Manu said, "John told him he'd transferred the money to another bank. I believe that's when Tim knew he was going to have to leave Tallulah Falls without the money."

"What he didn't know was that John didn't intend to allow him to leave Tallulah Falls at all," Reggie said.

"Yeah," I said. "Poor Mr. Enright could smell a rat but not the rubbing alcohol. So he tried to warn me. And then when he realized Mr. Langhorne must have put something in his Café Cubano, he tried to reveal Mr. Langhorne's part in Four Square." I sighed. "Too bad I didn't have an ink pen in that storeroom."

"I'm surprised he lasted as long as he did," Reggie said.

"The only reason he did was because he'd eaten just prior to going to the bank," Manu said. "Maybe he'd hoped John would have already left for the day and he could close out his account without a hassle. But John must've guessed what was coming after Lorraine left Tim, and he went ahead and prepared to transfer the money into one of his own accounts."

"Poor Mr. Enright," I said. "What a mess he got himself caught up in."

Reggie flattened her lips. "I think he had some big, redheaded help getting into that mess. Lorraine talks a good game, but she's a greedy woman."

"She did tell me she felt she drove her husband into his dealings with Mr. Trelawney," I said.

"Drove him, parked the car, and went around and opened the door for him," Reggie said.

"By the way," Manu said, "Chief Myers' brother-in-law had some shady dealings with the Four Square Development crew, as well, which is why Chief Myers tried to pass off Tim's death as accidental and Bill's death as a robbery. He didn't want the case reopened. He resigned today."

I tried to hide my smile. "Then Tallulah Falls has a new police chief? What do you two think of the guy who's taking over?"

Reggie patted her husband's arm. "I'm crazy about him."

Lorraine Enright, by the way, was able to get the bank to give her back the money John Langhorne had illegally transferred from their account. She's also still spending time with the private investigator . . . or, as Vera calls him, the Colonel. I guess Lorraine wasn't as broken up about Timothy as she'd professed. Either that, or spending time with the twin of a fried-chicken magnate is her way of coping.

I completed my Halloween haunted-house project and the Pacific Coast Collage. I've also made a little progress on the MacKenzies' Mochas logo for Sadie and Blake. But I still have plenty of time to finish that one. I'm continuing to work on Riley's bibs here at the shop. I haven't started on the baby blanket yet. I have a feeling Riley's commissions will continue up until and after her baby is born, because she comes in often to look at baby things and every time sees something else she absolutely has to have.

Speaking of Riley, I recently confessed to her that Sadie and I overheard her talking with Lorraine that night when we were leaving Mrs. Trelawney's house. I asked her why she was so adamant about finding out what Timothy Enright knew.

She bent forward and placed her elbows on her knees. "How would you feel if your father was in prison for a small role he played in something while the person who masterminded the entire scheme escaped scot-free?"

"I'd be pretty disgusted," I said.

"Yes, you would. I wanted to know what Tim knew. I wanted to know who Four Square Development's fifth partner was, and I wanted to see him go to prison." She sat back up. "Then when I told Dad I was having a girl, and the baby suddenly became real to him, he made me promise to back off. I guess in the end, John Langhorne got what he deserved after all."

"I guess."

Let me backtrack just a bit.

Vera had called Emma Langhorne, the other wife, which I thought went way above and beyond any normal social graces, and invited Emma and her sons to John's funeral. At first, she simply told Emma that John had died in a car accident. Naturally, the news media picked up the story, so Vera was unable to spare the boys the knowledge of how horrible their father had truly been.

Anyway, Emma brought her sons to the funeral. Since John Langhorne had turned out to be such a weasel, I didn't think anybody would show up.

I went, out of respect for Vera and out of gratitude, given that she'd possibly saved my life. Everyone else in Tallulah Falls must have had the same idea — the respect for Vera idea, not the saving-the-life thing — although I'm pretty sure everyone was relieved that Mr. Langhorne wouldn't be stealing from them anymore.

Blake, Sadie, Todd, Detective Nash, Manu, and Reggie were there. Everyone introduced themselves to Emma and her sons. Nobody mentioned their father; they just told the boys what handsome, capable young men they were and said Emma should be proud.

One of Mr. Langhorne's sons got teary-eyed and hugged me. I awkwardly patted his back until I felt him slip a piece of paper into the waistband of my skirt. I tried to back away, but he held me tight and, with beer-laced breath, whispered in my ear, "Call me."

As soon as he let go, I stumbled backward. Detective Nash caught me. "You okay?"

"I'm fine," I said. "I was learning that the rotten little apple there didn't fall far from the tree."

"Should I arrest him?" he asked. "Or just let Vera shoot him?"

I gasped. "What a horrible thing to say."

He laughed. "I'm only kidding. And Vera is well out of earshot. How's she holding up, anyway?"

"I have no idea. I know she's seeing a counselor Manu and Reggie know."

"That's good. She'll need a lot of therapy to get through this. And how are you holding up?"

I sighed. "I'm still having nightmares about the whole thing, especially about Mr. Langhorne coming after us in the Jeep and Vera standing there like a Bruce Willis, *Die Hard*-wannabe firing the gun at the windshield."

"I'm here if you need to talk."

"Thanks," I said with a smile.

"Me, too." Todd joined us. "I'm here if anyone needs to talk with me. Is this dark corner reserved, or can anyone join you?"

"It's reserved," Detective Nash said.

"Then let me steal your girl for a second. I need to speak with her," Todd said.

With a disgusted shake of his head, Detective Nash walked away.

"Was it something I said?" Todd asked.

"More than likely. What did you want to

talk about?"

"Riley . . . and Sadie . . . and you and me," he said. "Sadie said she told you that Riley and I used to date. That was years ago, Marcy, and I'm over it."

"I know."

"You know? Then why didn't you return my call that night?"

"I didn't return anyone's calls that night," I said, "except Mom's and Sadie's. I was tired."

"Is that the only reason?"

"That and the Four Square Development thing. You never explained why you rushed out on me after I asked you about the ledger."

He twisted his lips. "I had the same deal as Blake. I knew Trelawney was going to use my information. He paid me back by not charging me rent for a couple months." He spread his hands. "I have a friend who lost some money in a casino. He has a family to provide for, so . . ." He flipped his palms.

"Did Blake sneak around outside the Trelawney house after the break-in, and did you cover for him?"

"Yes. He saw a light on and thought the burglar had come back," Todd said. "And of course I covered for him. He hadn't done anything wrong."

"Why didn't you just tell me that?" I asked.

"Why didn't you *just* trust me?"

"Because we were *just* getting to know each other," I said.

"Can we *just* get back to that?" he asked.

"Maybe. *Just* maybe." I smiled.

ACKNOWLEDGMENTS

Special thanks to Jessica Wade, who made this book possible; Jacqueline Sach, formerly of BookEnds, LLC; and legal experts Glenn J. Null, Esq., John A. Cochran, Esq., and Rebecca Eller.

As always, thank you Tim, Lianna, and Nicholas for your unwavering devotion and support.